Chinawoman's Chance

A Portia of the Pacific Historical Mystery

JAMES MUSGRAVE

Edited by Cara Lockwood

Copyright © 2018 James Musgrave
All rights reserved.
ISBN: 9781943457311
Published at EMRE Publishing, San Diego, CA

DEDICATION

To all women and the Chinese-Americans who lived through this sexist and racist period in the United States and passed on the fight for equal rights and justice under the law to their children and friends in the generations to come.

Chinawoman's Chance

By

James Musgrave

© 2018 by James Musgrave

Published by English Majors, Reviewers and Editors, LLC

English Majors, Reviewers and Editors Publishers is a publishing house based in San Diego, California.

Website: emrepublishing.com

For more information, please contact:

English Majors, Reviewers and Editors, LLC

6784 Caminito del Greco San Diego, CA 92120-2219

Other Works by This Author

Forevermore: A Pat O'Malley Historical Mystery

Disappearance at Mount Sinai: A Pat O'Malley Historical Mystery

Jane the Grabber: A Pat O'Malley Steampunk Mystery

Steam City Pirates: A Pat O'Malley Steampunk Mystery

The Digital Scribe: A Writer's Guide to Electronic Media

Lucifer's Wedding

Sins of Darkness

Russian Wolves

Iron Maiden an Alternate History

Love Zombies of San Diego

Freak Story: 1967-1969

The President's Parasite and Other Stories

The Mayan Magician and Other Stories

Catalina Ghost Stories

Sign-up for the author's newsletter at
emrepublishing.com

Get a free copy of *Forevermore*, the international award-winning mystery, at any online eBook retailer.

Some Reader Comments

As they say, everything old is new again. In James Musgrave's *Chinawoman's Chance*, Chinese immigrants and women fight for liberty and justice in post-Civil-War San Francisco. Attorney Clara Foltz (a fictionalized version of the real person) gets sucked into the intrigue after a white prostitute is murdered. She and the detectives assigned to the case hope to save the Chinese man framed for the murder, which they try to do through derring-do and street smarts. –Kindle Customer

I found this such a very enjoyable well-written read, particularly since it was set in a place I have actually been & of which I know a little history. Mr. Musgrave is an ethical author and freely admits he has fictionalized real characters so you won't use this as a reference, but nevertheless, many of the main the characters were real people, well known people, of their times and may provoke some to look into the interesting details of their lives, so far as they are known. –Amazon Customer

Imbued with themes of racism and women's suffrage, "Chinawoman's Chance" takes the reader into the ghettos of San Francisco, the same ghettos to which Chinese immigrants were relegated with no country to call home. When a white prostitute is murdered, authorities don't think twice before arresting a Chinese immigrant. Enter Attorney Clara Folks, Suffragette, and member of the California Bar Association. Clara braves, not only Society's disdain, but threats of violence to prove her client's innocence and help find the killer. The ending is not one you'll see coming...No cliches here. –Kindle Customer

I received this book as an advance reader copy. My review is strictly voluntary and my own. This book highlighted the first woman lawyer of California's fight to break down the barriers for women and Chinese in post-Civil War America, specifically San Francisco. The history is fascinating; I had no idea how difficult times were for non-white and females. If you like history and a good story, this book's for you. – Paperback Reader

Table of Contents

ACKNOWLEDGMENTS

Although a work of fiction, this novel also uses facts and information from a variety of excellent sources. *Woman Lawyer: The Trials of Clara Foltz*, by Barbara Babcock, was one of my main sources for information about the hero of my mystery series. I must point out, however, that all of the plot is completely fiction. Also, historically speaking, Clara Foltz never defended a Chinese person, as she held with the attitude of the times that the laborers from China were a threat to workers in the United States. Clara also never worked with or even knew (as far as I could determine) Captain Isaiah Lees of the San Francisco City Police Department. Lees, however, was a real person, and another biography of his life and experiences can be found in William B. Secrest's book *Dark and Tangled Threads of Crime, San Francisco's Famous Police Detective, Isaiah W. Lees*. I also used many online sources to verify the setting of 1884 San Francisco and, especially, Chinatown of that era. The culture of the Chinese was also researched, and I apologize beforehand if I inadvertently used a source which is not factually correct. I often took dramatic liberties in portraying scenes and characters for story development.

I want to thank two women, one of whom is my first cousin, Kara Oh, for assisting me in the editing and "beta reading" of this novel. The other person is a Canadian named Jeanne Pawluk. Jeanne assisted me in the proper historical details of the Chinese cuisine and dress of this period.

"Whereas, in the opinion of the Government of the United States, the coming of Chinese laborers to this country endangers the good order of certain localities within the territory thereof. (Sec.1)" *Chinese Exclusion Act*, 1882.

Chapter One: Flayed

Jenny Lind City Hall, Police Department, Detectives Office,
Kearny Street, San Francisco. February 12, 1884

"I tell you, Captain, she was flayed like a dressed deer. Clean down to the bone."

Detective Sergeant Eduard Vanderheiden, or "Dutch" as his peers called him, was a tall, thin, bald, and agitated man with thick, auburn mustaches that curled on the ends like charmed snakes and flaming red chin whiskers. He also had a constant wink in his right eye. This nervous tic would often garner Dutch a drunken swing from a jealous husband's fist if he were seated within arm's reach of the Dutchman's chin. At age forty-nine, Dutch was never afraid to gawk at a pretty lady. That was his problem.

Captain of Detectives, Isaiah Lees, sat, manning the telegraph machine that connected each of the three San Francisco districts. Lees wore a brown frock coat and vest with checkered pants and spit-shined Oxfords. His face had the jowly redness of his fifty-four years, his hazel eyes were deep-set, and his brow was almost always in a contemplative frown. His graying goatee and full head of curly-brown hair were well groomed.

His one affectation was to wear a cape whenever he

2

was on a case, and, as a result, many of the beat cops sarcastically referred to him as "Pinkerton," after the bearded Scottish-American who founded the railroad's first group of private detectives. Captain Lees, however, was born in England and not Scotland, and he hated the railroads and their owners.

"Now that makes sense. Tongs use very sharp hatchets to enforce their will. I would wager she was probably keeping money from her handler, or else it was retribution for some other financial transaction. If twenty years in Chinatown taught me anything, it's taught me, money is the reason for everything." Lees stood up.

The First District of the San Francisco Police Department, with its station house at First and Mission Streets in Happy Valley, extended from California Street to Rincon Point. There was also a little lock-up or "calaboose" located in the First District station house. The Second District, with its station housed at City Hall at Pacific and Kearny, where Captain Lees and Detective Vanderheiden were now, was inside the former Jenny Lind Hotel, and it embraced the main business district. The Third District, with a station on Ohio Street, covered the area from Pacific Avenue north to North Beach.

Whenever a major crime was committed, the uniformed officer would send a message back to the Detectives' Office on Kearny, the Second District, and a detective would be dispatched to the scene. After the arrest, detectives took offenders to the main jail on Kearny.

"But she weren't no Tong girl. She was working at 814 Sacramento, next door to the rooming house. A white working girl. You know, most of the Tongs got their Chinawomen working over on Sullivan's Alley or Bartlett's." Vanderheiden pointed to a location on a large map hanging on the wall in back of the telegraph machine.

"Those white girls sometimes work alone. Who's at the crime scene? It might become dangerous." Lees picked up his holstered Colt .45 and buckled it around his waist. He felt for his Bowie knife behind his vest and attached his captain's badge to his cape, which was draped over the back of the swivel chair.

"Cameron was first on scene. Oh, and don't be surprised if Cook shows up. Cameron knows to notify the Chinatown Squad when there's a ruckus. This ain't no ruckus, but we know Tongs can start a war over much less." Dutch winked at Lees. He followed the captain out the door, and they rode the elevator from the third-floor office down to the street.

Inside the elevator, Lees scowled up at the taller detective, whom he had known for twenty years on the force. They had both been beat policemen after the Civil War and earned their detective appointments through hard work and many arrests.

"Jesse Brown Cook and his band of holy rollers don't understand how it is now that they passed the Exclusion Act. These Asiatics had no rights to begin with, and now that they can't get over here by boat, the competition between these men has escalated. I'm not surprised by this murder, and there will probably be a Chinaman behind it. But kid Cook gets his marching orders from Sheriff Connolly," Lees said.

"I seen Connolly call out the health team to fumigate every blasted gambling parlor, opium den, and hooker house in Chinatown. The mayor blames the chinks for every outbreak of typhus, malaria, and plague. But Connolly will poison the Chinatown rooms when the white kids in San Francisco so much as get the measles!"

4

Dutch punched into the air with his fist.

Lees smiled. "You know how the excrement rolls downhill? Leland Stanford, the pope of the bluebloods, says the Chinese are inferior humans. He never liked it when the coolies defended themselves against the Irish workers who attacked them while working on Stanford's railroad. And Stanford testified to Congress to get the Exclusion Act passed. He hand-picked Connolly, the Irishman, and Connolly picked Cook, the holy joe. The three of them think they're saving Christian America from the Yellow Peril. America's not supposed to exclude. It's supposed to include. Everybody!"

"Okay, Captain, I know where you stand. You're preachin' to the choir here. Just don't lose your temper with the kid the way you did last week when they fumigated the room where the baby was."

"That baby died, Dutch! All because of Cook and his band of holy rollers. But Cook was just the proximate cause. The underlying cause is men who think they're better just because they're rich, white and Christian." Lees returned the scowl to his brow, and they both stepped out into the chilly night air of San Francisco.

Detectives Lees and Vanderheiden walked the four blocks down Kearny to Chinatown. Once a crime scene was secured, they knew there was no rush. Unless suspects were reported on the scene, the methodical process of criminal detection would be usually slow and arduous. Witnesses, if any, needed to be interviewed. Evidence, if any, needed to be collected and classified. And, of course, the journalists were always there to provide a circus atmosphere.

Captain Lees had always enjoyed working the Chinatown beat. Sailing from his home in Lancashire,

England in 1848, he was an eighteen-year-old immigrant looking for adventure. When he landed in San Francisco aboard the *Mary Francis* on December 20, the Gold Rush had just begun. He worked as a laborer and engineer until he was drawn to the profession of law and order by performing a citizen's arrest when he saw a man stabbed for $300. He was hired by the newly established police department in 1854 and was promoted to captain four years later.

Now, as Captain of Detectives, Lees understood the social realities of being an immigrant in a strange land. Even though England was not China, he still believed the same fear and insecurities existed inside the men who came here to seek their fortunes.

Captain Lees had advanced in his chosen profession because he read a lot, and he was, like all good detectives, a student of human nature. He understood that humans joined groups to protect themselves from perceived threats to their livelihood or their person.

In a strange way, Lees himself had joined the police department because he felt threatened by the burgeoning greed of San Francisco during the Gold Rush. He witnessed men behaving like monsters. Raiding gold mining claims, killing the owners or stealing their gold— or both. When the railroad construction began, he saw how the owners, like Stanford, would speak out of both sides of their mouths.

On the one hand, they told the ruling class what they wanted to hear that America should be kept white. On the other hand, if they wanted to maximize their profits, the way Stanford did, they turned around and imported Chinese workers from Guangdong Province in southern China.

Lees knew these rich bastards were sly, however, in that they contracted with the governing Manchu in China, who forced the men in their country to become indentured servants. These immigrants had to wear the Manchu pajamas and distinctive queue pigtails and swear their allegiance to their rulers back home.

Lees wondered if Stanford or any of the other rich men ever thought about what life would be like if they had to forsake their civil rights, give up their families, and travel inside overcrowded steamships to a new world where they were accepted only by the greedy businessmen who would then run their lives and determine their fortunes? These Chinese had no human rights to vote, to organize, to marry, to testify in court or to even socialize with their superiors outside these Chinatowns.

Lees knew history. The first Americans were British subjects fleeing the Crown's persecution of their religion and their strange ideas about independence and freedom. They became indentured to profiteering "companies" in England who sent them to the New World under contract. Why couldn't men like Stanford see that these Chinese men were the same indentured citizens as their forebears had been? How was Buddhism any stranger than being a Quaker or a Catholic? Money! That's what changed their tune.

According to Lees, who was a pragmatic realist, most of the ills of a society and its persecution of minorities, could be traced to the unholy quest for profit at the expense of others. It had always been this way, and it was continuing in his beautiful San Francisco to this very day.

Lees had kept fighting these corrupt police and politicians, and he had no time for intimacy with anybody, even women. He spent his free time helping the downtrodden at the mission on Market Street, feeding them, and telling them stories about his crime-fighting duties in the city. He hoped the children, of all races, would find in him a role-model to maintain some balance in their otherwise turbulent and cruel lives.

Chinatown's twelve blocks of crowded wooden and brick houses, businesses, temples, family associations, rooming houses for the bachelor majority, opium dens, and gambling halls were home to more than 22,000 people. Even though the population had fallen after the 1882 Exclusion Law was passed, the atmosphere was still bustling and noisy, with brightly colored lanterns, three-cornered yellow silk pennants denoting restaurants, calligraphy on sign boards, flowing costumes, hair in queues and the sound of Cantonese dialects being spoken in the alleyways and outdoor markets. In this familiar neighborhood, Lees and Vanderheiden knew, the immigrants found the security and solidarity to survive the racial and economic oppression of greater San Francisco.

As they came up to the crime scene at 814 Sacramento, it was exactly 8 PM, and Lees saw that Cameron had roped off the front of the small door leading into the one-room apartment. Next-door, at the two-story rooming house, he could see several white women hanging their heads out of room windows, and they smiled and waved down at him and his partner as they ducked under the rope and shook hands with Officer James Cameron who was standing on the front step.

"Jimmy! You come up and see me after you're done, you hear?" One of the women yelled down, and Cameron's face reddened.

"Don't mind those wenches, Captain," said

Cameron. "They get a toot on with that opium, and you can never tell what they'll come out with."

"I know, Jimmy," said Lees. "Got anything for us?"

"No, when I arrived, there was just the body on the bed inside. One of the girls next-door knew where I was on my beat, and she come running up and told me about hearing a scream inside this little bungalow. You'll see exactly what I saw when I entered. Of course, I didn't touch a thing, but there was no visible weapon anywhere in plain sight. Only her gruesome corpse lying on that threadbare cot. No furniture. Just that bed and a small bedside table with a gas lamp. I tell you, Cap, I got sick to my stomach. I never seen nothing so horrible in me life."

"Do we know the murdered woman's name?" Dutch asked.

"Yes, it's Mary McCarthy. She used to live at the Methodist Mission for Wayward Women, but I guess she decided to ditch the straight and narrow and try to make some money on her own. Don't know if she had a handler, but it don't seem like it. I asked a few of the girls next-door, and they said they never seen no men, besides Johnny boys, escorting her to or from the apartment. As you know, clients come inside. Pimps escort their dollies around town and are usually dressed like peacocks."

Captain Lees opened the red door, and it squealed on its hinges. He stepped through, and the two other men followed him. The single gas lantern was glowing on a small table next to the cot. Lees motioned toward the lamp.

"Hold it over the body, Dutch. I want to inspect her," he said.

The tall detective gently grasped the bronze lantern by its semicircular guards and held it up over the cot. The bright light shone down on what was left of Mary

McCarthy, woman of the streets. In the corner of the room, the sound of what must have been a rat scurrying into a hole made Lees swallow hard.

Lees immediately saw that the face of the victim had not been harmed. In fact, he could still see the rouged cheeks and red lipstick, and Mary's green eyes stared at him accusingly beneath heavy blue eyeshadow and dark brown eyebrows. Her reddish-brown hair was piled high and fastened with ribbons and a silver seahorse comb. However, beginning at the nape, there began a horrific display the likes of which Lees had never seen before on man or beast.

Dutch's description of a deer flaying was hardly an acceptable comparison. The pulling from the outer epidermal layers was just the beginning. After removing the skin, the slayer had then removed all of the muscles, tendons, and intestines from the poor woman's corpse, until all that was left lying on the cot was the skeletal remains of a once lovely, nineteen-year-old orphan by the Christian name of Mary McCarthy.

Lees' eyes roved over the body like two searchlights. He stopped when he saw something exposed in the pelvic region, between the woman's legs. "Bag," he said, and Officer Cameron quickly took out a small paper sack, from a cloth container around his waist, and handed it to his superior. Lees bent down, reached out, and extracted a piece of thin lamb's skin from the orifice, and he gently dropped it into the bag. "Mark it as number 1, Jimmy," the Captain told the young officer.

"Looks like one of them new Sheiks. They sell for twenty-five cents apiece in the *Examiner*. Advertised as married women's friends. Ha! That Comstock Law's making a lot of rich businessmen," said Dutch, chuckling.

"I guess she had a customer before this happened. Something about him made her want to use protection." said Lees. "But there's hardly any splatter on the floor, walls or even on the cot. How did this butcher do it? And, more importantly, what did he do it with?"

"Maybe he was a butcher—a real one, Captain. We should investigate all the butcher shops in Chinatown. Maybe a Tong hatchet done this, but I think you hit the nail on the head. Only a butcher would know how to keep the blood from running like a river all over the place." Dutch shook his head.

"Yes, I think that's a good proposition. First, we'll run through my Rogues' Gallery of photographs to see if any butchers are there who've committed crimes. Then we'll go to the butchers without a record of criminal behavior." Captain Lees motioned for Dutch to put the gas lantern back on the little bedside table.

Outside, the Chinatown Squad wagon was pulling onto Sacramento with its loudly obnoxious siren and clatter of horses' hooves. Detectives Vanderheiden and Lees looked at each other and raised their eyebrows.

"Kid Cook," Captain Lees said.

"He will be cooking up something for certain," Dutch replied.

The door opened, and a tall, dapper, twenty-four-year-old sergeant entered, followed by three of his men. With a black-brush mustache, wide-set, piercing brown eyes and a commanding demeanor, he immediately took up position in the center of the small room. His blue uniform was ironed and spotless, and there was a yellow insignia of an Asian tiger stitched on his hat's crown.

"Gentlemen! I see you've secured the scene quite well, but now we can enjoin the real suspects. I'll question

11

Little Pete and Big Jim. They have most likely punished this lass for overstepping her bounds. You fellows know how these hi-binders feel about freelancers. Without getting protection money, they can become quite monstrous."

Captain Lees let out an audible sigh. "Jesse, my lad, you know as well as I that Fong Jing Tong and Chin Ten Sing are old men now. They haven't been active since the 1860s, and I would imagine they would readily confess to an assassination plot on Chester A. Arthur himself at this point in time. They are both senile, my good man."

"I can see you don't understand the ways of these pagan idolaters, Captain Lees. They worship their ancestors, and they always obey their wise elders. Sheriff Connolly has placed me in charge because I've studied their ways, and I've become quite proficient at weeding out the bad ones."

"At the grand old age of twenty-four, you've been able to cast a wide net of noxious fumes. I know. . ." Lees began, but Dutch grabbed his arm.

"Captain, I think we need to get back to the station and look over those photographs."

"All right, Detectives. We'll be keeping you informed. If I get a confession, I'll certainly let you know." Cook stepped over to the bed and looked down at the victim. "Oh, my! Would you look at that. Did you know, Captain, their Buddhist and Taoist religions require that corpse bones be shipped back to China for proper burial? Indeed. They also believe that the skin emits evil spirits, and so they will never handle a dead body until it's been stripped of the evil outer flesh. Our Christian coroners have been given that foul duty."

"I know all about the religious practices of the

12

Chinese, my dear Cook. And those Christian coroners get paid handsomely for their work. If you look closely, however, you'll see that this woman is not a Chinawoman. I'm not saying there might not be a Chinese connection here, but as it stands right now, I'm open to any suspect— Chinese or other races." Lees opened the front door. "Good night, gentlemen," he said, and he stepped out onto the front step. Dutch followed him.

Outside, the local newspapermen were awaiting them. They had the new dry plate cameras, and they were busy taking photographs of the scene and interviewing possible witnesses on the street. Now Lees and Vanderheiden were part of their picture-taking. One young man Lees knew as Boscombe, from the *San Francisco Examiner*, wearing a blue suit and matching derby, stepped forward, pen and paper tablet in hand.

"Any suspects, Captain? Find a weapon? How long has she been dead? Can we also get inside to get a photo of the body?"

Lees was surprised by the young reporter's last question. "Also? We have not allowed any person to come inside this crime scene, Boscombe. You know the rules. Nobody allowed in until we've gathered all evidence and questioned all possible witnesses."

"But there was a reporter inside earlier. I passed him on my way here. His name is Kwong. George Kwong. He's a reporter for *The Oriental*. He told me he got a picture of the white prostitute who was killed on Sacramento. His smile was wider than a Cheshire Cat's. When I got here, your man already had the rope up."

Lees knew that name. Kwong. Yes, that was the name of the leader of the Sam Yup Company, Andrew Kwong. Andrew also owned part interest in *The Oriental*, so that would explain how his son, George, got the job. Kwong was one of the Christian converts who got money from the Methodist Church to publish the only newspaper allowed in Chinatown. As the leader of the businessmen's company, he was probably the wealthiest Chinaman in San Francisco.

"As to your first three questions, Boscombe, no, no, and we won't know until the coroner gets here." Lees stepped past the gathered reporters, who were shouting out questions to him, which he ignored. From experience, Lees knew that no matter how he would answer the questions put to him, they would, most of the time, get transformed into something outrageous, to attract readership for their papers. Besides, Cook would certainly give them enough nonsense to fill their papers for weeks.

"I can see the headlines already, Dutch. INNOCENT CAUCASIAN DAMSEL MUTILATED BY BARBAROUS CHINESE RELIGIOUS CULT, or some such balderdash." Lees spat into the gutter. "However, I do want to meet with the Six Companies' leaders to investigate what they know about this murder—especially Andrew Kwong and his son, George. How did George get wind of this murder before anybody else? Why would that Christian rag want to promote the killing of a white woman?"

All around them, the noise of the Chinatown streets permeated the evening's glow, as the wispy fog began to creep across the pavement ahead, like the premonition of some curse beginning to cast its spell over the entire City by the Bay.

All of Chinatown and soon, most likely, most of Guangdong Province would be aware of the murder investigation. Kid Cook had taken it upon himself to arrest fourteen of the leaders of the Tongs. He had taken them to Sheriff Connolly's station, so Captain Lees was not informed until one of his detectives, Danny Carey, was over there because his best informer, Li Wong, had been arrested, and he discovered Wong was locked inside the jail on Kearny Street.

Lees knew the only thing really separating the Tongs and street justice was the sheriff's department. San Francisco had decades of vigilante law before the department was formed, and blood vengeance was still in the hearts of many citizens, as a holdover from the frontier and Gold Rush days.

Lees had learned to work with both the good and bad members of Chinatown. To the sheriff's department, however, the Tongs were always the bad men, never to be trusted. Lees knew better. There were Tongs he could work with to keep the overall peace, and they were much more valuable to him outside than they were locked-up. He also believed it was a better use of his time to follow the leads he had already uncovered in this case, especially the one that pointed to George Kwong, the son of Andrew Kwong, head of the Sam Yup Company. However, Captain Lees knew there was no such thing as cornering a man of his reputation. It would cause an immediate response from the entire community.

Therefore, Lees was going to arrange a meeting with all of the Six Companies' leaders at one time so that suspicions would not be raised. If and when he procured enough evidence to make an accusation or arrest, all of the leaders would be informed so that possible violence might be averted. Of course, Kid Cook and his arrests of Tong leaders had already placed all of Chinatown on high alert, and this was not good for Lees and his investigation.

Again, it seemed, Lees was fighting his inner foe: the conflict between his police department and that of the freewheeling and unrestrained Sheriff's Department that provided the captain with more obstacles than they provided assistance.

Once back at the Office of Detectives on Kearny, Captain Lees told Detective Vanderheiden to arrange the meeting with the leaders of the Six Companies in the morning. Before retiring to his apartment on Montgomery Street, Lees did a thorough search through his photographic records of arrested and convicted felons.

There were seven who had listed their occupation as "butcher," but none of them had a sexual assault or other such conviction. Two were arrested for larceny, one for assault, and four for drunken vagrancy. Only one was Chinese. Lees decided to delegate the questioning of these seven to one of his detectives, of which there were five, not including him and his partner. Perry O'Brien would probably be the best candidate, as he was not working on a case presently.

As Isaiah Lees leaned back in his chair with his feet on the desk, he thought about what questions he would ask of these leaders, and he remembered yet another connection to the victim. Mary McCarthy had previously been a member of the Methodist Mission for Wayward Women. He knew the woman, Rachel Benedict, the appointed head of that mission. She would need to be interviewed as well.

Finally, he also realized, Andrew Kwong received the money for his newspaper, *The Oriental*, from the Methodist Church in San Francisco. With those dots connected, the Kwongs became even more suspect. Was there perhaps some rivalry between father and son, which

16

had caused one of them to murder young Mary McCarthy?

Lees knew he needed to find out who had visited McCarthy the evening of her murder. Was it one of the Kwongs or some other member of the Six Companies? Did McCarthy perhaps begin to blackmail one of her clients? She was, after all, a freelance whore.

Of course, at this stage of the investigation, this client might have been anybody, and his hunch that this person was connected to Chinatown might be wrong. One thing was certain. The inscrutable way the Chinese could keep what white men called a "poker face," would be an added difficulty when he questioned them all at their meeting.

Chapter Two: Portia of the Pacific

Baldwin Hotel, California Street, San Francisco, February 13, 1884.

C lara Shortridge Foltz, age thirty-five and mother of five, was visiting her lover, Charles Gunn, age twenty-nine and a bachelor, when she was kidnapped by four Chinese men. Mrs. Foltz had met Mr. Gunn four years earlier, when she was serving as the first woman appointed Clerk of the California State Assembly in Sacramento. She had noticed the rather short but handsome young man with a full black beard standing in the front of the audience, smiling at her, as she spoke about women's suffrage to the mostly approving, mostly female gathering.

Minutes before the men in black silk pajamas broke into the room, Charles was listening to his lover tell him about the strange occurrence she had experienced the night before, around Portsmouth Square, near Jackson Street, in Chinatown. "I saw a man in the alleyway, and he was standing in the shadows leering at me. I was quite frightened, as I saw a flash of what I could have sworn was a blade of some kind in his right hand."

Mr. Gunn was immediately compassionate, and he put his arm around her waist as they stood together near the door. Charles had often heard Clara bemoan her condition as a woman left with five children, and he thought she sounded too unromantic most of the time. In fact, to the young politician, she sounded like Abraham Lincoln at Gettysburg, even when they were making love. Charles knew it was time for her to go back to her lonely room on Montgomery Street, and he was feeling sad.

"What did you do?" Gunn inquired, his voice a bit tired after their earlier lovemaking.

"I ran out of there, of course. I suppose I should have reported it to some policeman, but it was dark, and I knew this fellow had escaped. I saw him run off down the alleyway. Besides, just because he had a knife didn't mean he was up to no good."

"No, I suppose you're correct. You were wise to stay out of harm's way, my dearest," Charles said, giving his love another peck on her rosy cheek.

It was then that the four men burst through the door and confronted them both. One of the Chinese had a hatchet in his hand, and he waved it dangerously around. Charles, who was unarmed, attempted to stop the men from stealing his woman from the hotel room by shouting at the top of his voice to attract attention, but these men quickly formed an ingenious human arrow, with one man in front and three behind. They lifted his lover above them so that she was resting upon their hands in a vertical position, and they stormed out of the room, down the stairs, and out into the noisy hubbub of California Street.

Some passersby momentarily stopped and watched the strange procession, a woman in a fancy blue dress being carried by small but wiry men dressed in what looked like black pajamas. However, the Chinese were so fast and so efficient at dodging and weaving through the crowd that they were soon running down a side alley and out of sight. After running after them for a block, poor Mr. Gunn was finally out-maneuvered by the quick turns and adroit dodges, and he was thus left in the dust, standing on the sidewalk, waving his fist in anger.

***

All that Clara Foltz could think of as she was being whisked down the alley, headed toward Chinatown, was that her youngest daughter, eight-year-old Virginia, would have loved riding up in the air on the hands of four men. Clara herself was not unpleased with the experience, as these men were so competent at carrying her that she felt no discomfort. Somehow, after giving birth to five children beginning at age sixteen, in the rural wilds of Indiana and Iowa, this experience did not seem dangerous at all.

Even though Clara, a free love advocate, had procured the latest contraceptive, a gold wishbone stem pessary, an intra-cervical device, she was terrified about being raped. As long as she did not panic, and kept her wits, she believed she might even be able to talk her way out and survive this "bump in the road," as her grandmother used to call life's little adversities, such as tornados, dangers of childbirth with no doctors, and the attack from wild Indians on the plains.

As her entourage was clambering down the stairs inside a Chinatown building, however, the bumps became a bit much, granted, but the room into which they ultimately took her was quite large and filled with beautiful Asian decorations. Paper lanterns of almost every shape and size were lit, and, as they lifted her and let her slide—feet first—to the floor, she saw a row of stern-faced Chinese males staring back at her from behind a rectangular wood table of about twelve to fourteen feet in length and three feet high.

Perhaps her body was not going to be plundered for sexual gratification. However, she did believe all the anti-Chinese rhetoric, and she surmised that these men in front of her were in direct communications with the warlike Manchu profiteers back home. Again, she remembered the dark figure in the alleyway the night before and his huge, flashing blade. She shivered.

Mrs. Foltz often spoke in defense of Denis Kearney's Workingmen's political party, which was established in response to high unemployment and was in sympathy with the nation-wide railroad strike of 1877. This labor unrest, caused by the jobs taken by these Chinese, had even led to the infamous riots of that same year.

Clara had read about how the crowd back then had become agitated against these Chinese immigrants and went on a rampage that lasted three nights. The white men—mostly Irish immigrants--killed several Chinese, destroyed Chinese laundries, and raided the wharves of the Pacific Mail Steamship Company, which transported these dreadful Chinese to America to take jobs away from others.

But now, Clara observed six much different Chinese men sitting behind the long table, and all but one wore the silk robes, round hats, wispy facial hair and long queues down their backs. They looked the same as the men she had seen so often in the newspapers, both in photographs, and exaggerated in the political cartoons of the editorial pages. Only one man was wearing a western suit, with white shirtsleeves and tie, and he was seated in the center position. He began to address her in well-spoken English.

"I am very sorry for your rude transport, Madame Foltz. You see, we have been rushed into taking rather extreme measures. Let me introduce you to my compatriots, from your far left, and continuing down the line, we have Li Youchin of the See Yup Company, Wong Suh Woo of the Ning Yuen Company, and my name is Andrew Kwong of the Sam Yup Company."

Her host turned toward the gentlemen on his left and continued, "Next, we have Yueng Sheng of the Yeung Wo Company, Al Soo-Hoo of the Hop Wo Company, and Stephen K. Fong of the Hip Kat Company." Each one of the men bowed deeply as he was introduced.

"Thank you for your introductions, gentlemen, but as you are certainly aware, you are presently classified as kidnappers under the law. I suggest you explain the grave importance of this imposition upon my personal freedom and safety, as I cannot guarantee I will not prosecute you all when this is over." Clara was surprised that her voice sounded clear and confident. She may well have been addressing the California Supreme Court, if it weren't for those four rather ominous henchmen and escorts, who were still standing closely around her.

"I am happy to hear you mention the law, Madame Foltz. The main reason you have been brought here, under less than auspicious circumstances, is to retain you as our attorney. Fourteen members of our community have been arrested, and we have no means to defend them. I attended the trial you prosecuted in December 1880. I was impressed by your argument to the jury of all men about the guilt of the accused, Mr. Wheeler. You told them that you believed Mr. Wheeler's defense was not acceptable because he was trying to blame the victim, the sister of his wife, with whom he was having a love affair. He said he killed her and stuffed her body inside a trunk because she had asked him to do so. The victim was, Wheeler's attorney said, too embarrassed because a rival lover had found out about her relations with Wheeler, and she wanted to die."

Clara smiled, and she was relieved these men were not aware of her prejudices. She remembered the case well, as she and her female attorney friend, Laura de Force Gordon, were the first women ever to prosecute a murder case in a court of law. The publicity surrounding the case was good for her practice, even though the same basic prejudices existed at the time and would continue.

Many men believed that women could never argue to an all-male jury because they would "seduce them" with their wiles and feminine emotions. The prejudices she knew so well continued because of the legally established concept that a woman was a child, incapable of adult reason, and when she married, her civil rights merged into the protective custody of her overlord and master, her husband.

Oh. Yes, Clara knew personally about such "protective" husbands. Her Civil War veteran husband, Jeremiah Foltz, had abandoned her and her five children for a young woman in San Jose. To protect herself from society's harsh judgement against "sinful, abandoned women," she lied. She told everyone that her husband had died, and she was now a widow. At every turn, it seemed, Clara had to fight the male establishment to pursue her calling.

"Madame Foltz? Did you hear me?"

Andrew Kwong was talking to her. Clara cleared her throat.

"Yes, I did win that case, even though it was

23

adjudicated a mistrial because of another attorney who brought forth unacceptable evidence. However, I might add, the Defendant Wheeler was later retried and was hanged."

"And justice was served," said Kwong.

"Justice can be a cruel mistress, Mr. Kwong, as you and your fellows know so well. I must admit, I have been aware for some time about the way your people and other indigent poor are treated in our courts. I have even been working with others to propose a possible new office of the public defender, paid by the state, to address this flagrant imbalance in representation." She pointed at the American flag in the corner.

"Our Constitution's Fourteenth Amendment does say, after all, 'equal justice under the law,' but it applies only to persons born here. I believe it should apply to any person who is lawfully living and employed here because he or she must answer to the same laws that natural born citizens must obey. I must admit, however, that I have a certain personal prejudice about you and your people. Are you not part of the problem in our society instead of being part of the solution? Your business treaties are between your rulers, the Manchu, and our federal government, are they not? How can you demand your rights in our local courts?"

Clara wanted to be honest with these men. After all, she had never really explored their side of the immigration and civil rights issues. She wanted to know more about them. It was actually the first time she had voiced their side of the argument out loud, and the logic of it actually sounded very good to her.

After Andrew Kwong had translated what she said to his fellows at the table, they talked amongst themselves for quite some time. Finally, Mr. Kwong spoke for them.

"We believe you will help us because we are in a similar predicament as your other minorities, the Negro and the aborigine. We are also very like your majority, the female population. It is true, we are bound by our Manchu leaders back home because they negotiated the treaty which binds us in most of our contracts for employment in America. They are, as you said about your husbands, our lord and master. However, we, unlike you, must serve two masters. Not only are we bound by the contractual arrangement which we did not negotiate, we are also bound by your criminal and administrative justice systems, which we did not democratically approve. Therefore, can you wonder why we have needed to circumvent both masters to survive in America and have any future chance to assimilate into your society?"

Kwong straightened his necktie. "I have converted to Christianity in the Methodist faith and learned English, but I am not any closer to citizenship than my Buddhist and Taoist friends. Perhaps, I can mingle with the whites a bit more easily, but my civil rights are still forbidden. I have read about your Suffrage Movement. I understand you often take steps that are forbidden to you by the law, such as birth control and pressing the authorities for equal employment. You have forced the hand of the California legislature to permit women to be employed in the legal profession, have you not?"

"Why, yes, I and my sisters have accomplished this. We also argued successfully so that women can attend Hastings Law School. But I have not been able to attend because I must work to support my five children and my parents. I am still proud to see other women attend, however. Are you suggesting you and your brethren want the rights of American citizens? Do you hope to become citizens?"

Andrew Kwong answered quickly, "Yes. We would like to marry the female of our choice and have children. Why can't we be ordained citizens, even without a birthright? If we promise to uphold all the laws in these United States, then we should be granted citizenship, no?"

Clara was becoming more interested in the plight of her captors. Their argument equating to her cause of women's suffrage was a good one. How many years have women been virtual slaves to their master husbands simply because the American laws forbid women the right to vote and to enter into contracts on their own behalf? These poor Chinese have faced a similar dilemma.

"I like your argument. What is it you want me to do for you? How much are you willing to pay?"

Clara was a good negotiator. She knew the law of politics also. She had argued and spoken out for Republicans, Labor Independents, and Democrats. Usually, she was attracted by the party's specific stand on Women's Suffrage, but money had also often swayed her. She believed leaders in America were the ones willing to take a risk and speak out about issues that affected the population. Most followers were gladly willing to allow these leaders to speak for them, although sometimes it was to their detriment.

"Simply stated, we want you to argue for us in San Francisco criminal courts. Right now, fourteen men are being held without bail in your jail on Kearny Street. Tomorrow, we are being visited by Captain of Detectives, Isaiah Lees. He is investigating the murder of a Caucasian prostitute named Mary McCarthy. She was killed inside one of our apartments in Chinatown. The fourteen Tongs who were arrested are suspects, and I would assume Captain Lees will be looking for more. We want you here to represent us. We are willing to pay you the sum of one hundred dollars per hour for your representation." Andrew Kwong looked to his right and left, and the other men nodded their approval.

One hundred dollars per hour. Clara had never been offered so much money by anybody. Once, a wealthy dentist paid her to travel to the state legislature to get a bill passed which would allow him a refund of the money he had bequeathed the University of California. She had to fight him, tooth and nail, for every cent he paid her, and she ultimately had to take him to court to win a small judgement. That fiasco had taken up thousands of hours of her time and effort, living frugally on bread and cheese, and sleeping in the halls of the Sacramento Congress.

"Gentlemen. You shall have your representation. What time should I be here tomorrow?"

"Please be here before Captain Lees arrives at one in the afternoon," said Andrew Kwong.

"I will be here at noon. I have a lot of questions of my own to ask. The intrigue is just beginning, I expect. You can also be assured, gentlemen, that once Clara Shortridge Foltz is on your side, she becomes a tenacious tigress protecting her young."

When Mr. Kwong translated what she said, every Company leader at the table smiled, and Clara was pleased.

***

Clara had no escorts for her return to her lonely residence on Montgomery Street. She had moved into the small apartment after the dentist and his wife, with whom she had been residing while doing his bidding, cast her out.

27

She used the money from her judgement against him to rent her new place, wherein she also had her business office as well as her bed.

Her parents, Telitha and Elias Shortridge, still lived in San Jose with her five children. The goal she had was to make enough money to be able to move her family to San Francisco, but since the economy had taken a downturn, she thought that was probably not possible. But now, surprisingly, she was again invigorated with the prospect of making enough from the Chinese Companies to afford the move.

Clara had learned the law while working for a judge, Richard Warren, who was a friend of her father, from the time when her father practiced law. He merely sat her down inside his library and told her to study "the codes," as he called them, as well as the old books he had when he attended law school. Clara had poured over the rules and laws about contracts, criminal law, civil law, wills, torts, and compensation. Her father had early on recognized his daughter's gift for argument and her almost photographic memory.

But it was Clara's belief in herself and her abilities that gifted her with the initiative and drive needed to pass the bar on her first attempt. Even though she had not sat in a college classroom for more than one hour, she was able to become an attorney in California, something many men were never able to do.

If it were simply a matter of passing the bar, Clara's feat might not have been so noteworthy. However, she, along with her close friend and fellow attorney, Laura de Force Gordon, successfully argued with the California State Legislature to pass the ordinances which made it legal for women to pursue the profession of law, or any other profession, and to attend law school.

Although Clara wished she had the time and the money to attend law school, she now realized she had to put her mind and legal talents to work at providing the best possible defense for her new clients in Chinatown. What came to her first, as she walked along the breezy sidewalks of San Francisco, deeply inhaling the cool air, was the fact that she would need a different translator.

Even though Mr. Andrew Kwong seemed quite polite and educated, she knew his inevitable alliance would always be with his comrades. Therefore, he could not be trusted to always give her the truth. Clara realized she needed somebody to work with her who would not be biased. She knew of one Chinese who spoke perfect English, and who had successfully worked in a profession, albeit illegal, that was in direct conflict with the men.

Her name was Ah Toy, former prostitute and Madame, and the only Chinese woman to make it out of the confines of Chinatown and become a wealthy entrepreneur. Clara had successfully assisted her in suing a Tong leader who was trying to extort payment from her for his protection. When the 1854 Anti-Prostitution Law, aimed at the Chinese and not others, and the California Supreme Court decision in *People v. Hall*, which prevented Chinese from testifying in court, were established, Ah Toy retired from her brothel business. She began investing in real estate and took up residence in Santa Clara and San Jose.

However, Clara knew, Ah Toy was presently visiting San Francisco and living in the giant Mark Hopkins Mansion up on Nob Hill, the highest point in San Francisco. Mark Hopkins had been one of the "Big Four" owners of the Central Pacific Railroad, along with Leland

Stanford, Collis P. Huntington, and Charles Crocker.

Mr. Hopkins had died in 1878, so his wife and first cousin, Mary, was left with the property. She was a great lover of art and sculpture, so when Mrs. Sherwood Hopkins, age sixty-six, saw the many Chinese art objects that Ah Toy owned, she arranged for this meeting to buy some from her. Mary was not the typical "snob" on Nob Hill, so doing business with a former brothel Madame did not faze her one bit. Besides, most of her husband's fortune could be traced to the employment of cheap Chinese male labor, so Mrs. Hopkins was impressed by this attractive Chinese woman's success and determination.

Clara took the cable car, even though inventor Hallidie's wire rope did not assuage her fear. She held onto the seat in front of her for dear life, as she heard the groan of this rope being stretched while her clanging car mounted the steep incline on California Street toward One Nob Hill. The looming presence of the Victorian giant on the hill cast a shadow over her as she stepped down from the steps. To Clara, who spent most of her life in wood cabins on the Iowa plains, or crowded city apartments, it was quite monstrous. She had read that they painted all of the redwood to resemble stones.

This was the gaudiest mansion in all of San Francisco. It took up the entire block, and it was one mass of cupolas, turrets, and flying buttresses. Clara supposed there were also gargoyles hiding in the rafters somewhere leering down at her. There were dozens of balconies and bay windows, and if the mansion were white, it would have looked like one of those sugar confection castles seen in a Nob Hill bakery shop window. Instead, it was a very depressing gray-black.

As Clara walked up to the main gate, she saw the private security guard house. When a man armed with a Winchester rifle slung over his shoulder stepped out of the shadows, he startled her. "Madame? Who do you wish to visit?"

She supposed the guard was there because of the railroad labor strikes that were going on. When she looked closer at him, she smiled. He was wearing a gray-black uniform, including a ridiculous-looking British Bobby hat with a black plume sticking out of the top. "I'm here to see Miss Ah Toy. I believe she's a guest of Mrs. Hopkins."

"And, who are you? I need to communicate your identity up to the house."

"Clara Shortridge Foltz, Esquire. I don't think Miss Ah Toy is expecting me, but if you can contact her, I am certain she will vouch for our friendship."

The guard stepped back inside the guard house and returned momentarily.

"You may go up, Mrs. Foltz. Miss Ah Toy will be expecting you. Just tell the butler, Hannigan. He'll answer the door."

As Clara walked inside the gardens, she could look out over the hill. The entire City of San Francisco lay at her feet, and she understood why the wealthy wanted to be so high above everything. It gave one a God-like perspective. However, as she walked up the steps leading to the front entrance, the darkly ominous presence of the giant house cast a spell over her.

After raising the large brass ball knocker and letting it fall against the redwood, the door was immediately opened, and a short, thin and red-haired man dressed in black tails and a ribbon necktie, stood before her. "Mrs. Foltz?" She nodded. "Please follow me. I'll be escorting

31

you to Miss Ah Toy's room on the second floor."

The inside of the house was also dark, and she almost wanted to grab onto the butler's tails so she wouldn't get lost, but her eyes gradually became accustomed to the shadows. He took the stairs on the left, but before following him, she briefly looked down another gas lit flight of stairs in front of her. She could see that it led to the main drawing room below, and there were various paintings hanging on the walls, with two rows of benches for viewing the artwork.

The butler opened the door, and her old friend stood there to greet her. "Portia of the Pacific! My knight in shining armor! How are you, my dear friend?"

Clara knew not to hug the woman, as she was a reserved Chinawoman, raised in the old Chinese traditions. However, her speech was never reserved, as one would assume of a former "woman of disrepute." She was as tall as Clara, about five feet nine, and she had a respectful, sideward glance that made her brown eyes glisten when she raised her head to look at you.

The attorney also knew Ah Toy's clothing would be flamboyantly colorful and fantastic, and it was. She wore a long black silk dress called a *cheongsam* that extended down to cover her bound feet, and its front was adorned with an Asiatic, golden dragon, holding in its mouth an American eagle. The poor bird was obviously trying, quite unsuccessfully, to escape. Clara felt pristine and underdressed in her royal blue dress, with a slight bustle in the rear, that buttoned up to her neck in the front.

They sat together on the red couch with violet grapes adorning the pattern. Ah Toy's raven hair still shined, but it was graying at her temples, and there were white strands throughout the crown and down her pigtail.

She was now fifty-six-years-old, but she had few wrinkles, and her wide smile and dazzling white teeth could still captivate.

"Carrie, how is your most wonderful family? I trust they are healthy, and your children are attending the best schools."

Clara had never introduced Ah Toy to her family, but she had often told the Chinawoman stories about what they were doing. Ah Toy was one of the few people Clara allowed to call her "Carrie," her given name at birth in Indiana. Family given names were very important to the Chinese.

Ah Toy had begun her career as a seductress on her voyage to San Francisco from Hong Kong. Her husband had died on the trip, so she took up with the captain and become his mistress. When she landed in San Francisco, she had enough money to start her own harlotry business.

"Yes, my family is well. They are all staying in San Jose until I can save enough to move them to San Francisco. That is actually one of the reasons I have come. I now believe I might be able to make enough money to be with my family again." Clara leaned forward and grasped Ah Toy's hands. She searched her friend's face for a reaction.

"How wonderful! Please, tell me the details."

"I need an interpreter for a new job. Believe it or not, I am now employed by the Six Companies of Chinatown. They are paying me one hundred dollars per hour to represent them in their legal problems." Clara didn't know how this news would affect her friend, but she wasn't surprised when Ah Toy rose to the challenge immediately.

"Of course, you do! I know those slant-eyed

monkeys like the wallet inside a sailor's bellbottoms. I have a lot of time on my hands these days. Mrs. Hopkins is oh-so-slow to choose her art! I want some excitement, and now you have appeared. What will we be working on?" Ah Toy's brown eyes glowed.

"I am sorry, but I really don't have any very specific information at this point. The only facts of which I am aware concern a murder of a white prostitute who was killed inside one of the Companies' whore houses. Fourteen Tongs have been arrested already, and the Captain of Detectives, Isaiah Lees, will be meeting to question the leaders of the Six Companies tomorrow at one in the afternoon. Andrew Kwong, the English-speaking leader of my employers, was the only person I had to trust as a translator. That's why I've come to you."

"I know Andy Kwong. He has business interests all over the spectrum. Don't let him fool you, Carrie. He profits from all the sin trade. He just converted to Christianity to trick the white authorities. That newspaper, *The Oriental*, is a propaganda mouth of the Methodist Church. He runs that so he can run his whore houses, opium dens, and gambling parlors. He has his son, George, do most of the reporting."

"You see? That is why I need you as my interpreter. You not only speak the language, but you also have inside knowledge of the community. However, they are my clients, so my profession requires me to do my best to represent their interests." Clara stood up. "Can you meet me tomorrow at noon in the basement of the Tin How Temple? I can pay you for your trouble."

Ah Toy stood up and raised her right hand. "Stop! I will be there, but I don't need your money. I am an independently wealthy dowager, Carrie. When Mrs.

Hopkins buys my artwork, I will have even more money. I am doing this because I love you, and I want some excitement in my life again."

Clara was surprised when Ah Toy walked toward her, in her bound, mincing gait, and grasped her by the shoulders with both hands. "I missed you, my friend. You are one of the few women who never judged me because of my profession, and I want to thank you for that. I also thank you for including me in your new adventure."

"I know you will help me make the right choices. Even after what you told me about Mr. Kwong, I still believe he was sincere about wanting his people to have the right to become American citizens. That would include you, of course, my dear friend." Clara reached up and squeezed Ah Toy's hands.

"Hannigan!" Ah Toy yelled. "They have a pneumatic telephone to call the staff, but I prefer using my lungs." She smiled at Clara. "Besides, this redwood house is like one big echo chamber. Americans claim to be Materialists, and yet when they have beautiful materials, like the redwood used in this building, they want to cover it up and make it dark and sad."

"Be well, my friend," Clara said, and she walked to the front door. "I'll see you tomorrow afternoon."

"*Míng tiān jiàn,*" Ah Toy said.

"Which means?" Clara asked.

"See you tomorrow."

Chapter Three: The Meeting at The Joss House

Tin How Temple, Waverly Place, Chinatown, San Francisco, February 14, 1884.

C aptain Isaiah Lees liked to pursue a case in an orderly fashion. When he entered the temple on Waverly, accompanied by Detective Vanderheiden, he had his day of investigations all planned. First, he would interview the leaders of the Six Companies, then he was going to visit Rachel Benedict, head of the Methodist Mission for Wayward Women in Chinatown, and, finally, he wanted to visit the Mayor, Washington Bartlett, to plead with him to call off the Chinatown Squad arrests of Tongs.

Lees knew that if these Tong leaders were not released, there could soon be a war, which would not look good for the city's reputation.

Also, the Tongs acted as protectors of some in Chinatown who could not fight for themselves. Without their "security force in place," the population of Chinatown felt fearful, and they would react like a giant tortoise, withdrawing into its shell.

Tin How Temple was dedicated to the worship of the Goddess Mazu. She was believed to be able to protect China's seafarers as well as Chinese who were living away from home. Captain Lees saw that the Chinese head of the temple, Guan Shi Yin, was performing a prayer and spirit medium ceremony in front of the temple. Lees knew the

Chinese got very superstitious whenever something bad happened in the community.

The woman, dressed in an elaborate gold and silk robe and headdress, was the medium to receive Mazu's messages, and she was in a deep trance, shuffling around on the sidewalk. The black beads on the ends of a string, fastened to her headdress, were bouncing in front of her eyes as she nodded and shook her head. She was mumbling something in Chinese, and Guan Shi Yin, dressed in what looked like gold pajamas, was translating for her to the audience. There were about two hundred men in the audience, and they were clasping their hands in prayer and reciting something back to the medium, perhaps questions for Mazu or some form of thanksgiving.

"Think praying to Mazu will help get their Tong gangsters out of the hooskal, boss?" Dutch pushed through the crowd in front of Lees to get to the front door of the temple.

"Probably works as well as when you pray to the porcelain goddess after a drunk," Lees told him, making a mental note to question Guan Shi Yin. If the Tin How Temple was anything like Christian churches, he knew, there were a lot of sinners who went there to find a way to be forgiven. There were also religious fanatics, who had begun to believe God was telling them to do things. Either way, Lees knew, the Mazu curator would know if there was anybody saying anything about the murder.

***

Clara sat with her interpreter, Ah Toy, at a side desk that Andrew Kwong had set-up for them. Kwong had told her that he wanted an appearance of formal strength shown to the Captain of Detectives when he asked his questions. The six members of the Companies sat behind their usual

Clan table in front of which Clara had been brought the day before.

When Lees and Vanderheiden entered, Clara heard loud chanting coming from outside until the door was closed behind them. The two detectives seemed at first befuddled by the formal arrangement of seating, and they didn't know where to stand. Andrew Kwong pointed to a rostrum in the center of the room.

"Please, gentlemen, you may use that witness stand to ask your questions. It has a flat top for you to place your notebook." Lees glanced about and Clara thought he probably thought he was being tricked into intimidation by the group, but he didn't mind. He strolled over to the witness stand, and he took out his notepad from the inside of his gray cape and placed it on the flat top. He then turned to Dutch. "You have a pencil, Detective Vanderheiden?"

"Here you are, Captain," the taller man said, handing his superior a yellow pencil from his breast pocket.

"Now. Let's get down to the facts we know about this murder, and then I will begin my questioning. I don't think we need introductions, Andrew, but I would like to know the identities of those two attractive ladies seated on your left," Lees smiled, nodding at Clara and Ah Toy.

Clara thought that Captain Lees appeared quite a bit different than the police she had worked with when trying her only criminal case, *The People v. Wheeler*, in 1879. He looked a lot less formal, with his frock coat, cape, and checkered pants. His voice also had the hint of a British accent.

"I can introduce myself, Mr. Kwong. Captain, my name is Clara Shortridge Foltz, attorney-at-law, and this is my assistant and translator, Ah Toy. I have been retained to represent the interests of the Six Companies, and this will include advising them on their rights regarding your questions, if I may be so bold. Fourteen citizens of Chinatown have already been arrested by San Francisco sheriffs, so you can imagine why Mr. Kwong and his partners are concerned."

"Thank you, Counselor. It's an honor to meet you. However, as it is my duty to investigate a murder, which took place within one of the residences of your clients, my questions will relate to finding a possible murderer. I understand your concern for the welfare of the men who were arrested, but right now it is of no concern to me other than they might be possible suspects. At this point, anyone within reason is a suspect. The sheriff's department is in charge of their incarceration, and I suggest you take it up with them. Right now, I must find the killer or killers. Does that explain my purpose to your satisfaction?"

Clara felt like Lees was trying to handle her with kid gloves. She wondered if he knew her by name or reputation. "Yes, I will certainly contact Sheriff Connolly about their release. You may proceed with your questions." Clara believed her courtroom demeanor would assist her, as this policeman was obviously ignorant in the finer points of the law.

"Gentlemen, who owns the residence at 814 Sacramento?" Clara thought Lees wanted to narrow the search right away. If he could limit the range of suspects, it would improve his chances at finding clues as to possible connections with the victim.

"That is one of my properties, Captain," Andrew Kwong answered. "I rented it to Miss McCarthy when she came to my office and told me she had graduated from

Mrs. Benedict's Methodist school. She wanted to find employment, but she did not have the resources to pay rent for a place outside Chinatown. I am a Methodist, so I was sympathetic to her plight. I rented the apartment to her at five dollars per week."

"Were you aware that she was not looking for legal employment? In fact, she was working as an independent prostitute inside your residence, and had escaped Mrs. Benedict's home, not graduated." Clara studied Lees who watched the faces of all six of the men. She glanced at her clients as well. None, including Kwong, showed any emotion.

"I object. The rental agreement Mr. Kwong uses is legal and straightforward. It has a clause that stipulates that the renter can be evicted if she or he is discovered to be committing illegal acts on the premises. If he knew of this prostitute's activities, then she would have been immediately evicted." Clara responded as if she were talking to a judge.

"This is not a courtroom," Lees pointed out. "As you must be aware, Mrs. Foltz, laws are written mostly to protect the wealthy. In this instance, your clients. The reality of a cold-blooded and heinous murder, however, makes me a realist. For example, let us say there is a law against spitting on the sidewalk. It was written to protect the health and well-being of persons who use that sidewalk. However, this law is quite meaningless until an enforcer chooses to make the abstract words real by giving a citation to a violator. Excuse my vulgarity, but expectorant can flow like a river all over our sidewalks, but until a policeman acts, there is no law."

Lees walked over to stand in front of Clara and Ah Toy's table.

"I am one of those policemen who is trying to enforce the law against the willful and premeditated spitting on another person's life. In this instance, Mrs. Foltz, we are talking about a person who would not only kill this nineteen-year-old Miss McCarthy but who would then proceed to strip her body's skin and internal organs from her skeleton, leaving her unfit for a Christian Methodist burial."

Clara felt momentarily stunned. She hadn't heard the crime described in quite such details. Still, she tried to hide her surprise.

"Must you be so descriptive, Captain? You may proceed." Clara looked over at Ah Toy and raised her eyebrows.

"No, Captain, I was not aware that she was a prostitute. If I knew, then I would never have rented her the residence." Andrew Kwong turned right and then left, getting nods from his five colleagues.

"We all know who handles your dirty business, and many of them were arrested by the sheriff. You need to pay your bribes with more regularity." Lees wanted to get a rise out of them, and he could see by their reaction that he did.

"Our Tongs were arrested because there was a murder in Chinatown. My people become guilty before any evidence has been gathered. What kind of justice is that?"

Kwong's neck grew red.

"I agree," Lees said. "The Chinatown Squad wants to make a name for itself at your expense. I, however, want the truth." Clara felt surprised. This detective, indeed, wasn't like others she'd known. "Have any of your men ever had anything to do with Miss McCarthy?"

"Despite what you may think, Captain, the Six Companies does not maintain constant communications with our Tongs. We contract with them to keep our community safe. What they do on their own is not our concern."

"It should be, if what they do is run your gambling, prostitution, and opium interests." Lees crossed his arms across his chest. "But, never mind. What I want from you is access to all of Chinatown. I want you to communicate to your people that there is a murder investigation going on. I would also like to have your new lawyer and her translator accompany me. That way, you can be certain I won't step on anybody's toes."

"Of course. I will tell my people today, and you can begin starting tomorrow. Mrs. Foltz and Miss Ah Toy? Please arrange your schedules so you can accompany the good Captain."

Clara and Ah Toy nodded.

Lees stepped over to stand in front of Andrew Kwong.

"Before I leave, I would like to ask you and your son, George, a few questions privately, Mr. Kwong." Lees knew this was the time he could get into the real possibility of clues. The newspaper reporter had seen George going out of McCarthy's place on Sacramento shortly after, or possibly even before, she was murdered. The other members of the Six Companies were window dressing.

The elder Kwong spoke to one of the Six Companies directors in Chinese, asking him to contact his son, George, and tell him to come to the temple basement immediately. When the room was emptied of the others, except Clara and Ah Toy, Andrew Kwong let out a sigh.

"I knew it would come to this. You suspect me

because I am the wealthiest person in my community, and I also have assimilated into your society to the greatest degree. Murder, however, does not assist me if I wish to ingratiate myself further and become an American citizen."

Clara realized this was her chance to put Lees on the spot. She turned, eyes riveted upon Captain Lees. "Are you accusing my client of murder?" Clara sat up straight in her chair.

"Nobody is accusing anybody of murder until enough evidence is collected to prove such accusations beyond a reasonable doubt. This is the law, is it not, Mrs. Foltz? I am simply asking questions at this stage in my investigation."

"Very well. Just remember. If I believe my client's best interests would be harmed by answering one of your questions, then I will advise him not to respond." Clara looked over at Mr. Kwong until he nodded his head in agreement.

"Indeed. However, I would point out that if he doesn't respond to important questions, such as the one I am now going to ask, he will become even more suspect."

"I understand," Clara said.

"Mr. Kwong, where were you on the evening of February 12, between the hours of six and eight?"

Clara nodded at Andrew Kwong to give him permission to answer, but she was wondering if Captain Lees suspected something more than just the usual alibi responses.

"I was at home. My wife can vouch for my presence as well as my two servants. I retired that evening at ten, after going over some of the proofs for the next day's distribution of *The Oriental*."

George Kwong entered the temple basement. He was a tall young man of twenty-two, and his raven hair was slicked back and parted, in the Western tradition, and his conservative brown frock coat, white shirt, and necktie completed his business attire. His deep-set brown eyes moved over the faces of the others and stopped on his father's grim scowl.

"Father? You wanted to see me? What's all this about?"

"This is Captain Lees of the San Francisco Police Department and his assistant, Detective Vanderheiden. And these are the two women I told you about who are representing the Six Companies. The Captain wanted to ask us some questions about the murder of that prostitute on Sacramento two nights ago."

"I'm going to ask you the same question I asked your father. Where were you on the evening of February 12, between the hours of six and eight?" Lees knew what he would ask next if the response was what he thought it would be.

"I was at the paper finishing the galley proofs for the next issue." The young man didn't look at Lees. Instead, he kept staring at his father.

"I am afraid that won't suffice," Lees said, shaking his head. "You see, I have an eyewitness who says he saw you leaving the scene of the murder at approximately a quarter after seven. In fact, he told me you bragged to him about getting a photograph of the victim inside her apartment."

Lees studied the man. Clara could see perspiration begin to form on the young man's upper lip and forehead. She wondered why he was so nervous. Was it Lees' presence or did he have something to hide?

Andrew Kwong began to speak to his son in rapid Cantonese.

Ah Toy whispered the translation to Clara. "He's telling him not to answer any more questions. His duck is in the deep fryer. A Chinese expression."

Clara felt a sinking feeling in her stomach. Was she representing guilty men? She pushed the thought aside. She thought of her family. Clara had a job to do—for them.

"Excuse me, Captain. My client will not answer any more of your questions until you bring forth evidence of this alleged meeting," Clara said.

"I will be getting this testimony. I was simply giving Mr. Kwong an opportunity to be honest. The truth will come out, one way or another."

"Very well. Ah Toy and I will meet you here tomorrow morning at nine to go around with you on your detective hunt. If you would be so kind, please bring an affidavit from your witness about my client's whereabouts on the night of the murder."

"Thank you, Mrs. Foltz. I will bring such proof with me, and I look forward to showing you how a detective works at the street level."

Clara and Ah Toy were allowed to leave the room first. Clara was baffled by the captain's desire to have her go with him on his rounds. Perhaps, he just wanted to distract her. He seemed to be highly suspicious of Mr. Kwong and his son, George. She knew she was a novice when it came to detection and "sleuthing," as they called it. This Lees seemed a nice enough sort, so she believed she could learn a lot from him, even though he was on the other side. She liked his expression about murder. The taking of a human life is all that *should* be considered important. That's exactly the way she saw events when she was in the courtroom, so she thought well of this police captain who believed the same thing at the enforcement level.

***

After telling Andrew and George Kwong that they should not leave San Francisco until the murderer was found, Lees and Vanderheiden left the temple basement to go to their next interview. Lees believed the Kwongs were his prime suspects, so he wanted them close by.

Rachel Benedict was the Head Mistress at the Methodist Home for Wayward Women located in St. Louis Alley off Jackson Street. This was where the prostitute slave auctions were held when the girls of 10-16 were brought there by the Tongs to be displayed like prime cuts of meat and sold to the highest bidders.

Lees knew that Miss Benedict had purchased some of her "students" at these auctions, even though the church usually didn't have the money to do such things. He was going to ask her about this, along with more pertinent questions about the victim.

Miss Benedict's "school" was a converted bordello. It had a sloping, red tiled roof, with windows filled with colored glass images of different scenes from the Bible. Once inside, Lees could smell the odors of an abode that kept a clean and meditative sanctuary for young women who wanted to escape from the wildly carnal life that lay just outside, only a few doors down. Bath salts, lye soap, and rose fragrances combined to nip at his nostrils in a pleasant way.

Inside the main room, where the prostitutes were usually seated, waiting for their customers, was now filled with six Chinese ladies and one Caucasian, lounging in comfortable stuffed chairs, reading books taken from the

46

wide assortment of bookcases that stretched along the walls on three sides. This was obviously the room now serving as a library.

Captain Lees asked the one girl who was white and wore a long yellow dress with matching ribbon in her brown hair if she could tell Miss Benedict that Captain Lees would like to speak with her. The girl jumped from her chair like a jack-in-the-box, giggled, and ran up the stairs where the bedrooms were usually located. After a few moments, Rachel Benedict came down the stairs and into the library.

Miss Benedict was a short woman in her forties, with black hair, and brown eyes that took in all she surveyed with a calm austere gaze. She wore a simple dress of gingham and a white bonnet around her head. In fact, to Lees, she resembled a pioneer woman who might be a better fit riding some Calistoga covered wagon than working as a headmistress for a bunch of escaped prostitutes.

When she spoke, Lees heard a definite Southern drawl. She grabbed onto his hands and pushed them up into the air as if she were refereeing a prize fight, and she was declaring him the victor.

"O Captain, my Captain! What brings you to the Land of Milk and Honey? Haven't you always wondered how the Bible would use such feminine images for Paradise? Milk from the mammalian breast and honey from the female bee. My work, you see, is to get these little bees busy so they can return to society. Correct, ladies?" She withdrew her hands and spread them wide.

"Correct, Miss Benedict!" The girls shouted. "Bzzzzzzz!"

"Indeed. Now, Miss Benedict, if you will. I would like to ask you a few questions about the girl who was under your roof, one Miss Mary McCarthy." Lees raised his voice to bring down the frivolity.

The room immediately became silent, and Rachel Benedict frowned. "Mary was one of my best pupils. She worked harder at improving her body and spirit than any student I have had. She had escaped the pit of Hell, you see, and she wanted to be saved from that life. I tried to assist, but just when I thought she was ready to join the community of decent society, she vanished. Right after she got the highest grade on a geography test I had given."

"Did she say where she was going? What day did she leave your home?" Lees was working toward his primary question.

"No, not a word about her destination. It was on a Sunday. Yes, Pastor Reeves had given the sermon that morning, and I then gave the test. Sunday, the 10th of February." She cupped her right hand around her mouth and whispered, "Is it true what they wrote in the newspapers? Was her young body defiled in such a horrible manner?"

"I'm afraid so. Did anybody bring her to you? Did she have any visitors when she lived with you?"

Miss Benedict looked up to concentrate, and then she raised her right forefinger and smiled. "Why, yes! A young Chinese man brought her to me, and he would visit her from time to time. George, I believe his name was."

Lees' jaws clenched. "George Kwong?"

"How did you know? He was a fine young man. A journalist, I believe. He told me he wanted to save Miss McCarthy from a wretched occupation. He believed she was suited for a much better life."

"His employer, of course, is the same as yours, is it not? When the Methodist Church gives you money to buy girls at the auctions, is George Kwong or his father involved?" This was the point of Lees' questions.

"Why, no. I mean, I wouldn't know about their involvement. I am given money by the church elders with specific instructions to purchase the youngest among the girls, as they are seen as the most salvageable. There are so many Chinese men at these auctions, I wouldn't know if George Kwong or his father were there. Besides, it would be impossible to recognize them, even if they were there."

Lees, who had never attended these auctions, was still hoping he could place the Kwongs at the scene of such illegal business. "Impossible? How is that, miss? Do you not have good vision?"

"I have excellent eyesight, Captain. It's just that the bidders all wear masks. They are quite aware the authorities might be spying on them, so they disguise themselves. Of course, they pay the proper bribes, but every once in awhile, the Chinatown Sheriffs Squad will attend and arrest some of these scoundrels."

"Thank you for this information, Miss Benedict. If I have further questions, will you agree to see me again?" Lees motioned to Vanderheiden to get the door. They both moved toward the exit.

"Of course! I would do anything to help find such a monster. Although, God works in mysterious ways." Miss Benedict's brown eyes glistened.

"Yes? How so?" Lees opened the door. He could smell the foul odors of tobacco and liquors coming from the next door tavern.

"With a killer like that on the loose, my girls may think twice about the profession they've chosen." Rachel Benedict smiled and closed the door.

"Pretty smart dame, that Benedict," Dutch said, reaching into his vest to pull out a cigar. He lit it with a match he extracted from his watch pocket, cupped it in his big hands, and set the end ablaze by flicking the tip with his thumbnail. He held the flame against the cigar end, blew out the smoke, and grinned. "You think she's on the take at the auctions, boss?"

"Who knows? I'm not after the little fish, Dutch. I am going to press hard about George Kwong and his father, however. They look like the best suspects so far, don't you think?"

"Would seem so. Let's see what the mayor says about the Kwongs. Maybe he wants to clean up the city a bit." Dutch spat a flake of cigar tobacco into the gutter and hitched up his pants.

"Indeed. The excrement does roll downhill." Lees patted his partner's shoulder. "We need to follow the money."

As luck would have it, Lees and Vanderheiden were met by a man running toward them, coming from the direction of city hall. They recognized him as being from the mayor's office. Breathless, he stopped. He wore a dark suit and red tie with red suspenders, and Lees thought at first there might be another murder.

"Captain Lees?" The man was still panting. Lees nodded. "There's been a change in venue. The mayor wants you to meet him in Chinatown. He's dining at the Pagoda Inn on Jackson Street."

"Very well. Thank you, son. We'll head back there."

The office assistant turned on his heels and ran back up the avenue. Lees and Vanderheiden retreated back to Chinatown.

Inside the Pagoda Inn, the delicious odors made

Captain Lees' mouth water. He almost could taste the variety of dishes whose smells bathed him in their luxurious energies. Scallion pancakes, shrimp dumpling soup, Peking duck, shredded pork in hot garlic sauce, and chicken chilli. Lees and Vanderheiden often came to Chinatown to eat, as it was their favorite food. Also, many of their street informers were Chinese, so they never had to pay.

"Over here, gentlemen!" Mayor Washington Bartlett was waving from a booth in the back of the restaurant. Lees and Vanderheiden hurried over to greet him.

"*Buenos dias señores. Como estan ustedes?*" Among other things, including being one of the most prominent officials in San Francisco, who wanted all Chinese immigration stopped, Bartlett was also fluent in Spanish. He was a tall man, a former naval officer under President Andrew Jackson, a life-long Democrat, whose relative signed the Declaration of Independence. His hair and full beard were now all white, and the Six Companies in Chinatown called him "The Great White Whale," not in literary reference to Melville's novel but because he was wide of girth and brash of manner. Captain Lees found it more than ironic that the mayor dined so often in Chinatown, and yet still professed his racism at the table, but mostly in Spanish.

Lees and Vanderheiden squeezed into the booth. Bartlett pointed to the heaping mounds of rice, crackling orange duck, and other delights. "Enjoy!"

"Sorry, Mayor. We're working the McCarthy case right now. I wanted to ask a favor." Lees wanted to get down to business right away.

Bartlett filled his bearded face, with a shoveling

action of his chopsticks, from his bowl of rice. "Go on," he mumbled.

"Your man Connolly and his Chinatown Squad have arrested fourteen Tongs. I realize they might be suspect, but to get to the heart of this murder case, I need these men free and out in their community. Violence is bound to break-out if you keep them under lock for much longer, and then my case will become shrouded in anger. I won't be able to get an honest answer from anyone in Chinatown. You can understand my dilemma as a detective, can't you?" Captain Lees pleaded, aware that the motto hanging over Bartlett's desk read, "Honesty in Government."

Bartlett finished chewing, set down his chopsticks, and picked up the tiny teacup filled with oolong. He sipped and smacked his lips. "Of course! I will have them released right away. By the way, how is your case going?"

Lees was taken aback. He had not expected this, and now he was wary. Lees and Vanderheiden had always expected Bartlett to be in on most of the crime going on in Chinatown and that his racism was a way to cover it up from the public.

"Thank you. I'm just gathering testimony from witnesses. There are a few suspects, but releasing the Tongs will improve things substantially. I don't think this murder is connected to any gang rivalries or retributions. I have reason to believe, however, it may be related to something familial. Perhaps a father-son jealousy or something to do with a love affair gone wrong." This was the first time Lees had voiced his suspicions out loud. They sounded coherent enough.

"I know! As an old newspaperman, myself, I understand your concern. Would your suspects happen to be Andrew and George Kwong of *The Oriental* newspaper?"

Once again, Lees was astounded at the mayor's words. How would he know about Kwong? How had word gotten to him so quickly? "Why, yes, I just interviewed them both today. How did you know?"

"I have been in secret communications with them for six months now. I know none of you in the police force could know of this, but Mary McCarthy is not the first murder victim in Chinatown."

"What?" Lees looked over at Vanderheiden, whose eyes were now as large and round as the tea saucer under Bartlett's cup.

"Correct. There have been seven prostitutes killed—all of them Chinese—over the previous six months. When Kwong told me, I immediately knew this information could never reach the community in Chinatown. If so, there would be wholesale panic, and my administration, and even the Sheriff's Department and Chinatown Squad, could become suspect in their eyes. So, I have kept it under wraps. Until McCarthy's murder." Bartlett took another sip of his tea and licked his lips. "You might be interested to know that each of the killings had the same earmarks. The body was flayed and disgorged of innards, leaving the basic skeleton intact."

Lees swallowed hard. "This makes my case a completely different affair! I need a complete run-down on these successive killings. There is not one minute to waste!" Lees pounded his fist on the table, and the dishes and silverware rattled.

Bartlett's white eyebrows furrowed, and his grimace was vicious. "Listen to me, Lees. If my precious City of San Francisco became aware of these murders, can you imagine what would happen?"

"You might lose your job?" Vanderheiden said, and Lees punched him under the table.

"Not just that. The Committee for Vigilance still exists. If you think the Chinese riots were terrible, word of these murders would have people torching all of Chinatown! We must keep these murders out of the press until we solve this case. Is that understood?"

Sadly, it did make some sense to Lees, even though he was now mentally including Mayor Bartlett on his list of suspects. "So, are you going to get me the list of victims and all the evidence you have on these murders?"

"Of course, O Captain, my Captain! In fact, Andrew Kwong has been keeping all of this information for us."

Lees also thought about where he had heard that expression before. "O Captain, my Captain." Of course! The pioneer woman of the Home for Wayward Women, Rachel Benedict. Did the mayor know her? Were they having an affair?

"Kwong plans to write a detailed story for his readers as soon as we can find the murderer," the mayor continued. "Won't that be special? Let's just hope the murderer turns out to be Chinese. Otherwise, it may not be only my job at stake but yours as well."

Lees again slammed his fist on the table. "I follow clues and discover the truth! I don't give a hang who this killer turns out to be!" He glared at the man. "What you've done, Mayor, is a complete miscarriage of justice. Good day, Mayor."

"Oh, gentlemen," Bartlett called after the retreating officers' figures. They turned back around, and he said, "Keep this out of the newspapers, or you will be arrested as well. And you better both pray you find this killer soon."

"Oh, and why is that?" Lees asked.

"If the next victim is a person who lives outside of Chinatown, then you can imagine how the anger will escalate," Bartlett huffed.

"Indeed," Lees mumbled. "Hopefully, right up your mammoth posterior."

Isaiah Lees left the mayor, marching down Jackson with his partner, his mind chewing on the rising level of complication. This case wasn't at all what he thought, and if the mayor was right, there was an even more dangerous predator than he'd thought on the loose in his town.

Chapter Four: The New Investigation

Tin How Temple, Waverly Place, Chinatown, San Francisco, February 15, 1884.

When Clara met Captain Lees the next morning, inside the Tin How Temple basement, she was expecting a rather mundane police procedural. After stopping at the mansion on Nob Hill to retrieve her friend and translator, Ah Toy, they arrived at their destination at around half-past nine.

Once inside, Clara was surprised by a boisterous scene. There were a dozen policemen present, including Captain Isaiah Lees and his partner, Eduard Vanderheiden, and they had transformed the meeting room into an investigative headquarters. There were eight gruesome photographs affixed to the wall above the Six Companies clan table. They were lurid replicas of women who had been stripped of their skins and intestines, and their bodies were draped over chairs, on beds, and inside closets. These pictures also had arrows drawn, from one to the other, and beneath each photo was a physical description of the woman, including her name, the time of her murder, and the location.

"What happened, Captain?" Clara touched Lees on his gray cape, and he turned to face her. He was obviously preoccupied.

"I'm afraid this murder case has grown way out of proportion, Mrs. Foltz. I was informed yesterday that your clients have been hiding information about seven previous killings of prostitutes—all Chinese—which took place on different dates and locations during the last six months. This was a private affair between the mayor and the Kwongs."

Clara noticed that Ah Toy was standing on the other side of the room, under an ornate lantern, talking with Andrew Kwong. His son, George, was standing next to him.

"I can see that they all have the same operative details." Clara pointed to each photograph. "Do you suspect that the same assailant committed all of these murders?"

"Until I discover evidence to the contrary, I must assume so. The recent murder of Mary McCarthy seems to be a movement in a different direction, obviously. Also, the interval of time between each murder seems to be less." Lees pointed to the dates under each photo. "See? The first one was on August 17, the next September 12, then October 15. But then, from November 17 until February 12, three days ago, there were five murders committed, each one closer to the next by a week. At this rate, we might expect another one at any time. Oh, and here is the affidavit of the journalist who saw George Kwong on Sacramento the night of the McCarthy girl's murder." Lees handed the paper to Clara who tucked it inside her handbag.

Standing with a group of three men, including Jesse Cook, the Chinatown Squad leader, was Sheriff Patrick Connolly, a clean-shaven, red-faced Irishman, with curly-black hair, who was sporting a black frock coat with matching trousers, a vest, and white shirt and tie.

"So, you're the new lass Andrew was telling me about," Connolly said. "Don't pay attention to old Isaiah. His mind was fogged up in London, don't you know?" Connolly was in his thirties, and his accent was very Irish.

"Thank you for the advice, Sheriff, but I can think for myself. Captain Lees was going to show me the intricacies of his investigative technique, but now there seem to be many more cooks stirring the homicidal kettle, if you will." Clara was used to bantering with men, as she was the only female barrister in San Francisco.

"Somebody invoke my name?" Jesse Brown Cook called from across the room.

"Not that kind of cook, me lad," the sheriff said.

Clara knew that Captain Lees believed it was dangerous having Cook and Connolly in on this investigation, as there was probably a lot of money to be made for a leaked story. However, when Mayor Bartlett gave the order to release the Tongs, he had also decided to inform Connolly and his holy roller pal, kid Cook. Lees had decided to keep all of his findings a secret until he could uncover a suspect, but he would pretend to fully cooperate with Connolly and Bartlett to keep the peace in the ranks. The fly in his ointment was Clara herself. He needed her and her translator's help more than ever, and he was probably going to use it very carefully. He was going to work with her because he trusted her more than he did the sheriff and the mayor. In fact, Mayor Bartlett and Sheriff Connolly were, most likely, prime suspects in these murders.

"Sheriff, you and your men are going to question the Tongs about what they know concerning the seven murdered Chinese women. We need to know who they were dating and when, and then we'll need to compare notes to see if there are similar patterns at work." Lees took his Bowie knife from his vest and held it up. "For example, I immediately suspected the killer might have used a blade of some kind to do the flaying of his victim. I even had one of my men question butchers in the city. None of them was suspect, as they all had alibis as to their whereabouts at the time of McCarthy's murder."

"A blade is a blade, me boy-o. It's the sharpness and skill that matters," Connolly said.

Lees nodded. "Correct, Sheriff. But butchers also know how to dispose of the blood and intestines with the least amount of splatter and chaos. Each of these murders has an almost pristine crime scene, so where does that leave us with butchers?"

"Excuse me, gentlemen, but what about a coroner who must perform an autopsy? He or she would also have such grisly expertise. And, what about all of those who work in the burial services? They must also do such work." Clara was using her attorney's logic, and the men were paying notice. "Don't you think you should widen your net to include these types as well?"

Captain Lees frowned. He obviously hadn't expected Clara to divulge what he hoped to keep from Connolly and Cook. He was going to send them out to interview more butchers because there were now more victims. Now he would have to allow them to question coroners and funeral directors.

"Yes, well then, Patrick. Your men can make a list and begin questioning these types. Thank you, Mrs. Foltz." Lees nodded to the attorney. "I need to go now, and I would still like your assistance, Clara. May I call you Clara?"

59

Clara's face turned red. The captain should have waited until they were away from all these men before becoming so emboldened. "I suppose so. Ah Toy! We must leave with the captain now."

Stepping outside, Lees turned toward Clara. She was surprised at herself for being attracted to the much older man. Perhaps it was his calm, polite manner and English accent. Yes, but she supposed it was his sharp intellect that seemed to coincide with a deeper level in her own personality. When he spoke to her, his attention was riveted upon her eyes, something that other men rarely did. Other men didn't believe women were their equal, but this man did.

"Clara, you can follow me to see how I conduct my investigation. As the defense attorney, you'll be getting all this information eventually, anyway, and I'll be candid. I don't trust the mayor and the sheriff's department. They will not remain objective, and that's what I need right now: objectivity. Now that I have my own list of suspects, I will be proceeding to go back over them and ask more questions to narrow my search. However, there is one other person I want to question who is not on my list. He is the religious leader of this Joss House, the Tin How Temple. He speaks only Cantonese, so I will need Ah Toy's help as a translator. I would also like your legal expertise to help me assess any clues I might come up with later."

"Guan Shi Yin. He has been the minister of this temple for six years, I believe." Ah Toy looked up at the colorful frontage of the temple and sighed. "He took the name of the 'enlightened Bodhisattva' because the female figure could take any human form, both male and female. My people are very superstitious when they are away from

60

home. Mazu, Goddess of the Sea, has become a spiritual presence to pray to, and this man uses that need the way I used the female body in my business. In fact, here in the United States, she is called Goddess of the Heavens, a much loftier title."

"How can you compare a religious man with the business of prostitution? What he does is not illegal. In fact, religious practice is protected under our laws." Captain Lees frowned.

"That's right. Nobody gets hurt praying to a goddess, but I seen a lot of girls beat up by their pimps and Johnny boys." Dutch also had a scowl on his face. "And what about these here murders?"

"To some extent, I agree with you. The way the Hip See Tong conduct business does degrade the women and put them in danger. They treat them like animals, put them in cages, and let the men do just about anything they want to their bodies. When I ran my business, my girls mostly acted for the men."

"Acted? I don't get your reasoning." Clara thought Lees looked intrigued.

"She means she used feminine allure to make money, Captain," Clara put in. "We women have been doing this legally, in marriage, for thousands of years." She smiled over at her friend.

"Yes, nobody could touch one of my women. They could please themselves, mind you, and we provided accoutrements to assist them in this endeavor. I began by doing this alone, and I saw that it worked. I made more money dancing and showing them a gradual unveiling of my female form than I would have if I had to perform intercourse with each of them. Chinese men enjoyed my acting, as it coincided with our Taoist and Buddhist ways.

61

All of life, you see, is a drama produced by the inner God in all people, animals, and in all things."

"But you must have been approached by some men to do more than dance," Lees said, shaking his head in disbelief.

"Of course! But this was the genius of my approach, and it angered the Tongs. I was in control of whom I would allow to do this to my girls. I could carefully screen the applicant, if you will, so the danger to my employee was minimized. My girls received proper medical treatment, and they enjoyed their work. If they chose to marry one of these men, I would allow that also. The Tongs hated me for it, of course, and I eventually had to leave the business. My humane practice was too expensive to their way of thinking." Ah Toy raised the sleeve of her red silk dress to expose a long, jagged scar that extended the length of her left forearm. "One of them did this to me out of anger."

"My God! You never showed me that" Clara touched Ah Toy's arm and winced.

"Come, let's talk with the mystical man. Enough about me." Ah Toy climbed the steps leading to the temple's main entrance. The temple itself was on the third floor of the building. The second floor was where the clan associations met, including the Tongs. Lees could smell the odor of burning incense and perfume as he stepped into the room behind Clara and Ah Toy. Sergeant Vanderheiden held his nose and raised his eyebrows.

Inside the temple, the statue of Mazu sat on the central shrine with her assistants by her side. She was adorned in an Empress dress, all gold, and the ornate detail and jewels inserted in her belt were quite dazzling. Ah Toy pointed to the ceiling above the goddess's head. "Above the shrine are rows of red lanterns donated by devotees.

You can see the names of donors that are written on slips of red paper and attached to the lanterns. In front is a table full of offerings. The ritual items such as the joss stick holders were donated by devotees more than a hundred years ago back in China. For a donation, the worshipper may choose from this display of silver-colored seahorse combs, jeweled tie clasps, and small buddhas."

Dutch started to pick up one of the slips of paper to read it, but Ah Toy gently tapped his hand. "You must not touch. In fact, you are not supposed to be here. I suppose you were able to get permission because of the crimes, correct Captain?"

Lees nodded. "It wasn't easy. So, don't get us thrown out of here, Dutch."

"Okay, boss," the sergeant muttered.

"I see there are gifts for women on display. How many females come here to pray?" Clara asked.

"The prostitutes who are superstitious often come here to seek redemption from the gods or to ask for divine intercession," Ah Toy explained.

"I see," said Clara, and she wrote something down on her pad, which she had extracted from her purse.

Ah Toy continued with the tour. "The side shrines are dedicated to many other deities including Guan Gong, Justice Bao, God of Wealth, Wah To, Wah Kwong, Lady Golden Flower and eighteen Guardian Deities, Ji Gong, Lu Dong Bin and God of House Guard."

"You certainly know your gods, Miss Ah Toy," a deep voice came from in back of the shrine's red curtains. The draperies soon parted to reveal the temple minister, Guan Shi Yin, which meant, "hearer of all sufferings."

After Ah Toy translated the man's Cantonese, Lees assessed him carefully. His walk was austere and boldly confident, as this was his domain. As a lowly minister, however, his clothing was humble compared to his spiritual protégé. He wore a simple robe of gold that tied at the waist with a golden sash. He was tall, over six feet, and his face was dark and handsome. He had a cleft in his chin and an attractive mole on his right cheek. His straight, raven hair was pomaded so that it was perfectly symmetrical and parted on the left side with his queue hanging down his back.

Captain Lees knew Guan Shi Yin was thirty-seven years old and that before entering the clergy he had been in the funeral business, and his name was Joseph Fong. In fact, as he still had connections outside Chinatown, he made extra money from doing services for Chinese patrons who had the money to pay for burials. This was the main reason Lees wanted to question him, as there might be some connection between the burial business and a possible murder suspect who might work therein.

"Welcome. How may I assist you in your investigation, Captain?" Ah Toy's translation created a gap in time, and Lees spent it observing the minister's face. He looked sincere enough.

"Where were you on the night of February 12, between the hours of six and eight?" Lees figured he would establish his whereabouts first.

He spoke without hesitation in that sing-song chatter, and Ah Toy said, "He was performing a service in the temple."

"Good. Do you know if any of your—do you call them parishioners? Do you know if any of them have said anything about the murders of prostitutes or behaved in any suspicious way in your presence?" Ah Toy thought for a moment, and then she spoke to him.

Again, he answered quickly, and Ah Toy translated. "No, nothing was said about those murders. When I speak or perform a sacrifice, there is no talking allowed."

"I see. What about your services at funerals? Do you know anybody in your congregation who works preparing the bodies for burial or uses a knife of any kind in his job?"

Before translating Lees' words, Ah Toy explained, "Captain, we do not touch the body when it still has skin. The belief is that the flesh has evil spirits, so we employ white men to do the work of stripping off the flesh. The body is then ready for burial, but we most always send it back to China to be buried with the relatives."

"Thank you, Ah Toy, for that information. I would still like to know if he knows anybody who does this stripping work, whether they are Chinese or white men." Lees knew the sheriff's men would be asking these people also, but if Guan Shi Yin knew anybody, it would save time.

The minister paused for the first time before responding. Ah Toy finally translated. "He says he knows many such men, as he used to be in the funeral business. However, because the work they did is seen as disgusting and servile, he never wanted to know them personally."

"I see. I also saw a woman who performed in the street outside as the psychic medium for your goddess. What kinds of questions or requests does she receive from the men?"

After Ah Toy translated, the minister smiled broadly, and his response was quite long. Finally, Ah Toy offered the translation. "They ask many things. For good health, for a good woman and companion, for a safe trip back to China, or perhaps even to get rid of some specific disease or bad habit. Mazu can create the dance of the gods

65

inside a person so that any problem can be solved."

"Wonderful. And I would expect you get paid handsomely for your part," Lees said, but when he saw Ah Toy shake her head in the negative, he rephrased his words. "I mean, thank you for your help. If I should need it again, would you be open to more questions?"

Ah Toy translated Lees' last words, and Guan Shi Yin again smiled that spiritual grin of his and answered, "Yes, anytime, Captain," Ah Toy translated.

When the group was down the stairs and standing in the street again, Lees confided his assessment. "I want to talk about motive right now. Why would a murderer want to commit a series of killings right under the noses of thousands of Chinese? What do we know about these victims? Now that the mayor and the Kwongs have turned over the details of the other seven victims, I know they had one thing in common, besides the fact they were all prostitutes."

"What's that, boss?" Vanderheiden asked.

"They were all independent prostitutes. This means they were a direct affront to the Tongs and their sex traffic business. I was, at first, angry with Connolly and Cook when they arrested the major Tong leaders, but now I'm not so certain. Could one of them be involved in these murders?" Lees buttoned up his cape, as it was beginning to get cooler.

"I don't think so," Ah Toy responded, buttoning the top button on her red silk *cheongsam*.

"Dear, I think we better get you inside. That flimsy garment won't keep you warm," Clara said. She was hoping the Captain might get the hint.

"Come with me. There's a nice Italian restaurant over on Stockton. It's just a few blocks." Lees began to lead the way.

Clara smiled and nodded at Ah Toy. "See? Chivalry is not dead. Even in the police force."

***

At Mona Lisa's Ristorante, inside a back booth, all four investigators were huddled together, sipping espressos, and chewing on breadsticks, waiting for their dessert orders to come. Lees sat next to Clara, on the right, and Ah Toy and Vanderheiden were next to each other on the left side of the booth.

"Please continue, Miss Ah Toy. Why is it you believe the Tongs would not want to kill these women?" Lees asked, nibbling at the end of his breadstick.

"I know the Tongs and how they do business. They are ruthless, yes, but they are also pragmatic. They see these women as their product, their source of income. Even women like me, who work alone, are not a threat to their business because we attract men with more money from outside Chinatown. The Tongs who deal with prostitution also deal with gambling, alcohol sales, and opium use. As long as the lone prostitute encourages her client to make full use of the sins available, they never get pressured, much less murdered. I was a threat only when I became a Madame. That made me a fellow business entrepreneur, so I was pressured to leave, but they would never have killed me."

"Show them your scar again," Clara said.

Ah Toy pulled up her left sleeve, and the men frowned. "Yes, I got cut as a warning, and I chose to leave. However, if I had decided to play their game, and give them regular tribute and protection money, I could have stayed in business. I was ready to leave, anyway. I made a lot of money in those fifteen years of work in Chinatown.

67

I was given a Chinawoman's chance to succeed."

"Yes, and that was more of a chance than she would have been given outside Chinatown," Clara said, sipping her tiny cup of strong Italian coffee.

"True, and that leads me to another suspect. Again, this person probably wasn't the murderer, directly speaking, but he could have hired such a person to commit these atrocities." Lees lowered his voice. "Mayor Bartlett hates the Chinese. He got elected on a platform of supporting the national Exclusion Act. And now, from what I hear, he wants to run for governor in the next election. Wouldn't his chances improve greatly if there were wholesale murders being committed in Chinatown? Why, Dutch and I were with him today, and he said as much. Didn't he, Eduard?"

Vanderheiden looked up and saw the waiter bringing the tray of desserts. "Wait up, Captain. I want to taste my Cannoli before I say another word." He selected the dish with the sweet cheese-stuffed funneled treat. He picked up his fork and took a big slice and pushed it between his lips. "Oh, boy, that's better than a gift from Mazu herself!"

The others were given slices of Tiramisu coffee cake, and they all ate silently for a few moments, enjoying the experience.

"Sure, the mayor could get a lot of good press from all of these murders. He did tell us he hopes the killer is Chinese. And he threatened our jobs if we found out the killer wasn't a chink—excuse me—a Chinese." Vanderheiden licked his fork.

"How ghastly! I never realized there was this kind of racist subterfuge going on at high levels of our fair city," Clara said, but she was purposefully coy. She played the

68

same "innocent female" in the courtroom. It allowed men to open up even more to expose their weaknesses.

"I received another clue from Miss Benedict at the Home for Wayward Women. There were two clues, but the second may be a coincidence. First, Miss Benedict stated that George Kwong was the man who brought Mary McCarthy into the school. He would also visit the girl from time to time. The second was the fact that Benedict used an expression for me when we first met. She called me O Captain, my Captain. Coincidentally, the mayor called me the same name, and he had never done this." Lees dipped his fork into the cake and held it there. "I wondered if Benedict and Bartlett might be having a personal relationship."

"That was from Walt Whitman's poem about the death of President Lincoln, was it not?" Clara asked.

"Yes, it was. Frankly, I was wondering if it might not be a veiled threat. Assassination being the operative word." Lees picked up the fork and brought the cake to his lips. He held it there.

"You mean, if Bartlett and that woman are working together to get these girls murdered, then they might also be planning to take you out if you get too close to the truth," Clara said. "Has our corrupt society come to this?"

"But why would they want the bodies of these women disfigured? It makes no logical sense." Ah Toy wiped her mouth with a cloth napkin and then set it down.

"It makes sense if you realize Bartlett once owned a newspaper. The more sordid and fantastically morbid a murder is, the more readers want to buy it. It's the old saw of when a dog bites a man, it's not news. But when a man bites a dog, it is." Lees took the forkful of cake into his mouth.

"And if these murders get solved under his watch, and the killer is Chinese, then the White Whale gets his votes for governor. The story would certainly become state, if not national news," Clara pointed out.

"Yes, and that's the sum of my thinking. Of course, there are still George and Andrew Kwong and their involvement in this. Could they be the proximate murderers? If Bartlett paid them a lot of money, they could become killers who would profit from the case behind the scenes." Lees was thinking out loud. He trusted Clara Foltz with this information because he believed she also wanted to find the truth. After many years of fighting the mayor and his private sheriffs, he had finally realized he needed to show somebody what was happening in this city that was preventing real justice from prevailing.

"Captain, I realize you know where I must stand on this. These two men are my legal clients. I must represent their best interests. I am, however, thankful that you are sharing this with me." Clara smiled over at Lees, and he returned the grin.

"You two should get a room!" Vanderheiden laughed, and he drained the last of his coffee.

Sergeant Vanderheiden escorted Ah Toy back to her residence on Nob Hill, and Captain Lees did the same for Clara Foltz. This small team had become closer during the day, and Lees wanted to express his gratitude in a more personal way.

"Clara, I know you didn't get any money today by spending your time with me. Do you think you'll be able to pay for your family to come to San Francisco?" Lees stood at the bottom of Clara's apartment building on Montgomery Street looking into her eyes with his usual direct gaze. Gas lights were lit along the street, glowing with a reddish hue in the fog. Lees was not anxious to go home to his lonely flat, and he wanted to know more about this fascinating woman.

"Thank you for your concern, Captain. I am being paid quite handsomely by the Six Companies, and yes, I do believe I'll be able to soon afford to get my parents and my children back into my arms. I do miss them so. The world of the law, as I know you can appreciate, can be quite arid and without humor. My children make my life joyous and exciting, even though the stress can be of a different variety, if you've spent any time with young ones." Clara smiled. She could tell by the concern on the officer's face that he was a gentle man. He reminded her of her father, Elias. He was the one who steered her toward the law, but it was his spiritual quality as a pastor that reminded her most of Captain Lees.

"I'm afraid I have little experience with the wee folks, except when I'm called to a home that has family trouble." Lees took hold of Clara's hands as the fog rolled in.

"I love to cook, sew and do all of the family things we women were raised to do. My mother, bless her, does this now for me. I became a Suffragist when I had to compete with men for a job. I realized we women had the right to work in any trade we were qualified to practice. I saw that if the laws needed to be changed, I could do the petitioning to change them. If nobody did it, then I had to do it. I also discovered many women who would help me compete because they had been deserted by husbands also, either through death or divorce, it did not matter."

"I agree. These prostitutes, for example. If there were more jobs open to women, then this type of work would soon become less appealing." Lees squeezed

Clara's hands, and she returned the pressure.

"Yes! And I know you are under pressure for your legal convictions. My father, who was once a pastor before becoming a lawyer, used to preach the heretical doctrine of soul-sleep."

"Soul-sleep? That sounds quite profound. What does it mean?" Lees asked.

"It means he believed when a person dies, his or her soul does not go directly to God. Instead, it does not exist until the day of the Last Judgement, when all souls are called to argue before their Maker."

"That makes some logical sense. How can one even have a Last Judgement unless all souls are there? If God judged each soul or spirit, when the body died, then there would be no need for a Last Judgement at all."

"I knew you had the same kind of insightful intelligence as my father. It does make perfect sense, but all the Protestant and Catholic religious leaders did not see it that way. Probably because they couldn't tell their parishioners they would get into heaven right away, and this caused consternation and perhaps no tithing at all. Therefore, father was excommunicated to the backwater revival tents, where he still likes to preach, from time to time, even as a lawyer."

"Jolly good for him," Lees said, then bent forward and gave Clara a kiss on her left cheek. She could feel the foggy dew from his mustache, and her face reddened.

"Captain! You must come to the station." From out of the fog, Sergeant Vanderheiden came running up to them. Lees and his partner made it a practice to share addresses whenever they had to split up.

"Slow down, Dutch. What happened?" Lees could see by his partner's face that this was important news.

"Sheriff Connolly has made an arrest for the eight murders. He's got him locked up now at Kearney Station." Vanderheiden was still huffing and puffing, bent over and gasping out the words.

"I told him to wait until we could compare notes! Who is it? Who did he arrest?"

"George Kwong. Connolly says he has enough evidence to convict and have him swinging from a rope on Russian Hill."

"I must go with you, Captain. George Kwong is now my client," Clara said.

"Of course! We must all leave right now. I want to see this so-called evidence for myself. I also want to see what kind of pressure the sheriff is getting from the mayor."

Chapter Five: The White Whale

Jenny Lind City Hall, Police Department, Kearny Street, San Francisco. February 15, 1884

It was twenty past midnight when Clara and Ah Toy arrived at the police station on Kearney. As Clara suspected, Andrew Kwong was there, sitting on the long bench in the squad room. Uniformed sheriff officers and city policemen were busy booking new criminals. Mr. Kwong stood up and waved. "Mrs. Foltz! Over here!"

Clara and Ah Toy walked over and sat down next to him on the bench. The attorney noted that her client's eyes were red from weeping or, perhaps, a head cold. He spoke with his usual enunciated and perfect English, however, and there was no congestion.

"They won't show me anything. My son was arrested in the middle of the night, and now I can't see him, and they won't give me any details about how he could have committed these brutal murders. You have to help me!" Mr. Kwong grabbed hold of Clara's dress sleeve with his right hand and pulled as if he could get a response from her by trying to break her arm.

"Please, Mr. Kwong! Let go of me. I'm here now. I understand your problem, and as your authorized counsel, it's now up to me to find out everything. By law, as George's defense attorney, they must provide me with every piece of hard evidence, and each witness they have that they believe proves your son's guilt. He is not guilty until they can prove, beyond a reasonable doubt, inside a courtroom and in front of a jury, that he killed these women. I will do my best to counter each piece of evidence and rebut every witness."

After Andrew Kwong released her, Clara gently patted his hand. "Please, wait here. I'm going to first meet with the arresting officer, Sheriff Patrick Connolly, and then I will meet with your son. Right now, I don't want you in the room with us, but I will bring you back later when we have to mount our defense strategy."

Ah Toy spoke to Andrew Kwong in Cantonese, and he nodded his head and spoke to her vehemently.

"What did he say?" Clara asked.

"He said it was the White Whale who did this," she told Clara.

Clara wondered who this White Whale could be as she walked over to the desk sergeant. She was asking him about meeting with Sheriff Connolly, when Captain Lees came up to her, grabbed her arm, and spun her around to face him. "I can't talk to you here, but I'll meet you later in the afternoon at your apartment. Is that clear?"

"Yes. I will be expecting you," Clara said, and she watched Lees turn and dash off to the other side of the squad room.

"Go down that hall and turn right at the last door. The sheriff's expecting you," the desk sergeant instructed her by pointing toward a long corridor on the right side of the building. "Walk right in. You don't have to knock."

Inside the sheriff's office, Clara felt as if she had stepped inside a menagerie. There were at least fifteen different animal heads peering down at her from the mahogany walls: bears, mountain lions, deer, and one rhinoceros. Connolly was seated in back of his high desk, leaning back, his hands behind his head, a big cigar in his mouth. He wore the uniform of the Chinatown Squad, so she assumed he had arrested George Kwong, her client.

"We meet again, Mrs. Foltz! Please, take a seat." Connolly pointed toward a small wooden chair near a long bench on the side of the room. Clearly this room was not meant for the comfort of visitors.

"I would prefer to stand right now, Sheriff," she said. "I'm representing the Kwong family in this case, and I need to see George. But first, I want to know what you have on him. I don't need the actual evidence right now, but my legal team will need it eventually. I just want to be aware of what we may be up against here."

Connolly blew a perfect large smoke ring, then blew a smaller one that pushed through the center of the first. "Your pal Captain Lees did a lot of the work to nail this kid. He got the sworn testimony of Boscombe, the journalist who spotted George Kwong at the scene of the McCarthy murder. I was just putting two and two together. I interviewed a coroner across the Bay in Oakland. Name's Goodbody, a fine name for a coroner, and he informed me that Georgie boy worked for him for a whole summer. He told me the lad was especially interested in how to use the U.S. Army post-mortem field kit that Goodbody used. In fact, when we arrested the lad, we found it hidden under his mattress. George Kwong quit his job suddenly, and he took the kit with him. I asked the Oakland doctor whether his little kit could strip a body down like that of Mary McCarthy, and I showed him the photo of her body. He's willing to swear in court that his kit could be used for such purposes."

"All right. I'll eventually need to see that. Of course, that does not prove my client used it on anyone. What motive do you have? What witnesses saw him use it, or what reason would he have to kill those women?" Clara was fishing for clues in Connolly's demeanor. How confident was he concerning all of this tommyrot about George working as a coroner for a summer? Young men need money—especially young Chinese men—and there weren't many jobs that they were allowed to do.

"We talked to Miss Benedict at the Methodist Home for Wayward Women. She says Georgie boy had a big row with his girlfriend, Mary McCarthy, and it was a week before she was killed. Oh, and by the by, we won't be pinning those seven other murders on your boy-o. He may have done them in too, but the mayor wants to hold off." Connolly took another deep drag on his cigar. "One murder conviction will be enough with a white jury, don't you think, Mrs. Foltz?"

Clara was livid. Without the reality of those seven other crimes, she had little with which to fight. She knew no Chinese court testimony was allowed in a courtroom, they weren't considered citizens, and she wanted to use that fact to support her client. Also, what evidence could they provide to prove his hatred for his fellow Chinese women? This single murder of the Irish girl was different.

"This changes things greatly, Sheriff. I want to see my client right now."

"Right. Now don't be getting your bustle in a bunch. I'll take you to his holding cell." Connolly stubbed out what was left of his cigar into an abalone shell ashtray on his desk. He led the way down the hall and out into the squad room. "Smith, I'm taking Mrs. Foltz up to see her client."

Clara followed the two men upstairs where the jail cells were located. She could smell the foul odors of urine and feces, and she could hear the grinding noise of old plumbing. George Kwong's cell was in the back where the Chinese and Negroes were kept.

Smith opened the door with his key, and Clara stepped inside. It was dark and shadowy, lit by a small gas lamp with a protective shield of wire mesh, and it was sitting on a table next to a threadbare cot. George Kwong wore the blue dungarees issued to all prisoners, and his last name was stenciled above his shirt pocket. He stood up when Clara came in, but she motioned for him to sit back down on the cot.

"Your father is outside. I'll soon see to it so he can visit you. How are you feeling?" Clara placed her hand on the young man's shoulder.

"I didn't kill anybody, Mrs. Foltz! I was in love with Mary McCarthy, but she wanted to do things on her own. She didn't think she was lovable. We argued about that, but I never threatened her." Clara could see tears glistening on the young man's cheeks. "I worked for Mr. Goodbody because I wanted to learn a new trade. I don't know how that post-mortem kit got in my room. Somebody must have placed it there."

"All right, George. I'm going to ask you a series of critical questions, and I want you to give me an honest answer. Whatever we share is privileged and protected information. However, if you lie to me, even once, I will refuse to represent you from that moment on. Is that clear?" Clara watched him nod his head.

"Were you and your father working for Mayor Washington Bartlett or anyone else in city government?"

"No, the mayor just wanted us to keep the Chinese

prostitute murders a secret. He was an old newspaper publisher, and he told us we could make a lot of money by keeping a record of all the details and photos, but we must not publish anything until he gave the word."

"When did he tell you this?" Clara wanted to pinpoint the actual progression of this most significant negotiation.

"After the first murder. Father was ready to publish the story in *The Oriental*. But then the church officials said to hold off. They said the mayor wanted to see us first. He came down to Chinatown and told us he would put his best men on the case, but he wanted us to keep the murder a secret. When the second murder happened, he again visited us. He said if this story got out into the community, there would be fear and anger generated in the populace, and Chinatown could be invaded by the Vigilante Committee and others. He said his men had to find the killer before we could tell the story, so we agreed."

Clara knew this information agreed with what Isaiah Lees had told them at the Italian restaurant. There wasn't much more she could do until she heard from Lees. She needed to get all the evidence from Connolly before she did her own investigation.

"I'm going to go get your father so he can talk with you. I'll meet with you both tomorrow so we can plan our defense strategy. Right now, I need to go home and get some sleep. Everything will be taken care of, George, so don't panic."

"If I were guilty, I would panic, Mrs. Foltz. Right now, I'm just afraid." George's dark eyes were staring at her with a fixed concern.

"Afraid? What scares you?" Clara took his two hands into her own.

"I'm afraid that when news gets out that I've been arrested for murder, then some person who knows about the other seven killings will try to profit by selling the stories to the press. When that happens, the entire city will be after me."

Clara could see George was in a real panic. He was perspiring profusely, and his voice was trembling.

"It's happened before, and the police could not stop them from executing mob justice on the men involved back in 1856."

Clara could feel the young man's hands shaking. She knew the case about which George was referring. She had to study it for her bar exam. These members of the Vigilance Committee later became the People's Party.

In fact, Clara belonged to the Workingmen's Party, which evolved from the People's Party, because of their support of the Women's Suffrage Movement. She spoke for their candidates, including Denis Kearney, who became its leader.

Clara understood why George and his father would be concerned. They, too, were involved in criminal activities in Chinatown and were newspaper men, just like Charles Cora and William Casey back in 1856, who were holding onto a story that would cause violent repercussions throughout the city.

Finally, the mayor himself was involved, and he was going to soon run for Governor of California. If Bartlett decided to deliver his story to the press about the seven other murders, then Andrew and his son, George, could easily be seen as the Charles Cora and William Casey of 1884. Their knowledge of the murders would make them guilty, even without a trial.

Chapter Six: A Woman on the Hunt

Montgomery Street, San Francisco, February 15, 1884

Inside her apartment on Montgomery, Clara was about to fall asleep when she began to think about her defense strategy to keep George Kwong from the gallows. The power of the press was important. She used it to speak out for women's rights and other issues. What if those other seven murders were leaked—not by Mayor Bartlett's office—but by Andrew Kwong and his church-supported newspaper, *The Oriental*? She wanted to discuss this further with Captain Lees when he came by later. She fell asleep thinking about Lees' dewy kiss late the previous evening, and she smiled.

Captain Lees appeared at Clara's door promptly at nine. She let him in wearing her tennis dress, a striped affair with her corset loose and her bustle small. Unlike her peers, Clara did not feel pressured to constrict her circulation in order to affect the narrow waisted, big bustled look. After giving birth to five children, if a man expected a virgin's hourglass shape then he was delusional. The pleasant smile and fixed look of intelligent interest on the officer's face was enough for Clara to understand he was not impressed by outward feminine appearances.

81

"Clara, I must talk to you about George. I spent an hour with Connolly, and he wants to get this to trial very soon. We must …"

"Please, Isaiah. May I call you by your given name?" Clara interrupted.

"Yes. Certainly, but …"

"I have had my own discussion with the sheriff. In fact, I wanted to pose a strategy I have in mind to defend George. I know you come from England, where the press is forbidden by law to give out details of a criminal investigation. In this country, however, as you're now certainly aware, since we have a constitutional form of government, we place much more value on the free press being able to get the facts out for its citizenry—even before a case has gone to trial. The First Amendment was added for that purpose."

Clara watched Lees walk around her apartment gazing at the decorations. She had posters of her speeches at various political rallies and gatherings around California, and the main poster, right above the couch, was one that showed her with Governor Robert Waterman who was congratulating her on the passage of the state law that gave women the right to work at any trade or profession, and this included going to law school and taking the State Bar Examination.

The rest of the display, on hanging shelves, showed photos of her family and her five children. There was also some framed artwork depicting San Francisco and its beautiful landscapes and cityscapes. A long bookcase filled with legal books was decorating the wall next to the small kitchen. She saw that Lees had little interest in the furniture, but he could see her taste was very provincial, except for the purple couch. A stuffed, high-back chair, a footstool, a birdcage with a canary, and a table for tea and coffee service were the practical pieces. No flowers, no frilly doilies or coverlets, no ostentatious European antiques. This was the domicile of a working woman.

"Yes, I know the difference. We at the station call the newspapers the circus because of how they exaggerate the facts. What does your defense have to do with the press?"

"I believe what you said about Mayor Bartlett. He wants to win the governor's race, and he's willing to use the Chinese to do it. The only way he can cause a calamity big enough to attract attention is to arrest George, convict him in a virtual kangaroo courtroom, and then hang him with great hoopla in the press. I want to prevent that from happening."

"As it just so happens, I agree with you. I went over what Connolly has on Kwong, and it's mostly circumstantial. No weapon, no witness who saw George murder the girl, and testimony that reeks of bribery. I still think Bartlett is in cahoots with Miss Benedict the bee lady at the Home for Wayward Women. She could be in on his rise to power." Isaiah Lees took hold of Clara's hand. "Now what's your plan, Clara? Maybe I can help."

Clara moved over to her purple couch and sat down. She patted the cushion, and Lees followed her lead and sat down beside her.

"I am going to help Andrew Kwong write an article for publication. He will not only publish it in his paper, *The Oriental*, but I will take it to all the major papers in San Francisco. This article will explain the facts behind all seven different murders that took place in Chinatown and how Mayor Bartlett was the operational force behind keeping them a secret from the public." Clara squeezed

Lees' hand, and he squeezed back.

"I think it's a good plan. The only way you can prevent Bartlett from using these murders to get him elected is to tell your story. Also, this could have an additional advantage."

"Additional advantage? What do you mean?"

"The murderer is still at large. When this story becomes public, the killer will become enraged. I believe these killings may have been used for political purposes, but that doesn't mean the killer is able to be bought. A certain blood lust sets in after several such murders, and the added ingredient of sex lust makes me believe this person will strike again." Lees stood up. From inside his cape, he extracted a small pistol. It was a 45-caliber double-shot model of the small Derringer. "Keep this in your purse. Use it if you need it."

Clara looked down at the pistol in her hand and sighed. As a wife and mother in the wilds of Illinois, she used a weapon to hunt or to ward off predators. This, very personal weapon, was a new experience, and she knew it was meant to kill a human being, the highest order of mammal on Earth. No matter how uneducated or primitive, a human life was sacred. Her parents and her culture raised her to believe this, but now she was being told there were exceptions in the world of police work.

"Thank you, Isaiah. I hope I won't have the opportunity to use it. When I go down this path, I do understand I will be exploring the darkness of mankind, and I respect your experience and your assistance. I now must do it alone."

Standing at the door, Clara stared at Captain Lees. His intense gaze made her believe he was able to see a deeper, intangible beauty within her. She forgot about the little Charles Gunn and his political aspirations at her expense. Lees gave her a dignity that caused her to stand erect, with her back and shoulders set in a firm, immovable position. And yet, she knew, there was a humble and motherly aspect to the slope of her bosom down to her corseted waist, and his eyes followed that path.

Clara allowed this roaming of the eyes from this man, this older, wiser, and battle-tested man. Her first husband had been battle-tested, even wounded, but the experience had weakened him and had made him afraid to be a real man. This male before her, with his concentrated scowl and piercing gaze, had been wounded mentally many times as well, she knew, but he had become stronger and kinder, with a passionate need that she could see was authentic. When he kissed her, she moved into him, and afterward, as her head rested on his shoulder for several minutes, perhaps the length of time it takes to clean a gun, she felt stronger after she withdrew.

***

Later, inside the office of *The Oriental* newspaper in Chinatown, on Waverly Place, Clara Foltz was seated before the desk of Andrew Kwong, the editor. As she spoke, she could see he was distraught, and deservedly so, as his son's neck was virtually encircled by the heavy weight of a legal system that despised his kind.

"Mr. Kwong, I want you to use the information you have collected about the seven murders of Chinese prostitutes in order to show the population of San Francisco that Mayor Washington Bartlett has been using you and your community to advance a political agenda. Indeed, as we have discovered, he wants to run for the office of California Governor, and it has been his intention to do so from the moment he stepped foot in your office

85

aftcr that first murder." Clara could see a glimmer of hope in the man's eyes.

"Of course! That's why he arrested George. He knew George would be at every scene of the crime to take photos, and so when the white girl was murdered, he had what he wanted. And you say we should explain these facts in an editorial?"

Clara stood up and walked over to stand in front of Mr. Kwong. She stared hard into his dusky eyes and her smile was just as dark. "I want not just an editorial about what the mayor is doing to you and your people, I want you to explain what can now happen to all of San Francisco if we don't find the real killer of these women."

Andrew was listening intently to her words. His eyes were riveted upon her face.

"I want you to ask all of the women of the city to write in to explain their fear of being struck down by this predator, and I shall be the first woman to answer your call. I will explain to them why I believe my client, your son, is innocent. I will also tell them I am acting alone as the hunter of this heinous monster, because the mayor doesn't wish to expend the resources to find him. I am alone in my hunt, a woman in the wild, if you will, and I want them to demonstrate against City Hall to show their support for me!"

Andrew Kwong winced. "But, Mrs. Foltz. What if this killer is not captured in time? What if he doesn't kill again? Don't you believe the mayor will go ahead and hang my boy anyway?"

"This murderer doesn't necessarily have to kill again. That is another reason why I am circulating this article of ours beyond Chinatown. I want to enrage the killer so he comes out of hiding. I am going to ask more questions of the suspects we have in mind. I hope to narrow the list to one or two main suspects. Once I know whom to track down, it will be simply a matter of trapping him or her before he or she can kill again."

"How will you do that in so little time? Russian Hill and the Vigilantes are also waiting." Kwong pointed out.

"Don't concern yourself. I believe I now have the bait that will lure this killer out of hiding and into a trap."

"Bait? Another woman? Who would be insane enough to tempt the hand of this monster?"

"You are looking at her," Clara said, and she turned around, walked to the door, and left.

***

The article ran in all the major newspapers in San Francisco, and the national edition of the article ran through the Associate Press and the newer United Press. Eventually, because of the telegraph, all major newspapers had published the story about the woman out West who was confronting the male establishment in order to prove her client, a Chinese man, of all people, innocent.

Because of the danger to attorney Clara Foltz, and the obvious political corruption of the mayor, readers were sympathetic to her plight and were less suspicious of the arrested defendant, George Kwong. Indeed, when they read about how seven murders had been kept secret by the mayor, and George Kwong was a lowly journalist taking photos of the crime scenes, the women became embittered toward the San Francisco legal system.

After they read Clara's letter that explained how she was hired by the Six Companies to protect their business interests in the community, and then she had to protect the son of its most learned and religious owner, Andrew Kwong, they were livid.

87

Women from all over the United States began to learn that these poor Chinese had no rights in a court of law or in society. They were trapped inside their ghettos of poverty, and Mr. Kwong had converted to Christianity and was trying to save the souls of these poor women being held prisoner in the wicked flesh trade of Chinatown.

Not only were these women's lives being threatened by the acts of Mayor Bartlett, the entire female community was also in danger. Where would this killer strike now? He or she had already broken the racial divide and killed a white girl. Who would be next? It could be any woman in San Francisco! If women could be so easily struck down, what might happen in the communities of any state in the union?

After one week, this single editorial had elicited thousands of letters to the editor, and the demonstrators began to arrive in San Francisco by the trainload. They filled the hotels and rented rooms in the homes of enterprising homeowners, and they met at the churches and in the parks of the city to plan their demonstration against the mayor and City Hall.

***

City Hall, San Francisco, February 22, 1884

Inside the City Hall auditorium, Mayor Washington Bartlett was standing in front of his assembled cadre of uniformed sheriffs, police officers, and newspapers sympathetic to his cause. In addition, Captain Isaiah Lees and his partner, Detective Sergeant Eduard Vanderheiden, waited quietly in the back of the room, subservient yet observant, as the leader of the city droned on.

"I want a full cordon of police presence around this building immediately! I have already responded to that scurrilous editorial, and I want my response circulated on all the press wires around the country. These Chinese and this one woman have usurped the law, and I will not allow a potential murderer out of my jail! The safety of my city must come before any special interests of criminal aliens who care not a whit for our culture or for our system of justice. This is why we keep them out of the country. They have stolen jobs from our good men, and they have brought crime and ungodly practices to our shores."

A few of the sheriff's men shouted their approval. Bartlett grinned back at them.

"I will speak to this crowd of women, and we shall have our day in court! This man, this Kwong, will be hanged if our evidence convinces the jury, and no outsiders will ever sway the method of American justice that has withstood our Revolution against the British, and the many martyrs of our Civil War will have not died in vain."

Bartlett's voice became louder, and his face was red. Sheriff Connolly yelled, "Hang 'em high!"

The mayor continued, "America is for Americans, and we have no room for foreigners who have made their deal with the big business tycoons of New York, behind the people's backs. This foreign treaty has been disavowed once and for all, and these interlopers and pagans will never set foot in this great city, or in any other United States territory or state, ever again!"

Captain Lees and Detective Vanderheiden looked at each other and shrugged their shoulders. Vanderheiden took a cigar out of his jacket pocket, held it under his long nose, and smelled it. "Is Foltz out questioning the suspects?"

"Yes. She told me she has her own ideas about who

might have committed these murders, but she wants to narrow down the list." Lees shrugged again. "I gave her the Derringer. What else can I do? She's a hard-headed woman."

"She better not shoot the wrong person, boss." Vanderheiden laughed.

"What do you mean, Dutch?"

"Bartlett ain't going to let her roam around without somebody trailing her, now is he?"

Lees scowled. "All right, you've convinced me. I will make certain she has a clear path to discover what she called the evils of mankind."

Captain Lees knew he was risking his job by allowing this woman to have so much information and trial evidence. However, it was his many years of antagonism that had made him do this. Seeing the vigilante hangings, and then watching the sheriffs become an unfair substitute for this kind of knee-jerk, biased justice had become too much for Lees to stomach. He hated the mayor and his group of private vigilantes called the Chinatown Squad more than he feared losing his job, and he was going to let his natural sense of practical judgement overrule his ego for once in his life.

***

For the entire week, Clara and Ah Toy visited all the main witnesses that Captain Lees considered suspects. Clara, of course, was beginning to have her own idea about who might have committed the murders, but she wasn't certain she wanted to share it as yet. To her way of thinking, proving that the mayor had or had not hired this killer was not relevant at this juncture. Most important was the fact that another woman could die at any moment, and she wanted to prevent that.

She had first questioned Rachel Benedict at the Methodist Mission for Wayward Women in Chinatown. Clara found the woman quite eccentric in her ways, but her answers had been forthright. Had George Kwong ever struck Mary McCarthy in her presence? No. Had he threatened her in any way? No. Had she seen the two youngsters engaged in any affectionate activities? Yes, they often sat and held hands, staring into each other's eyes, and George seemed quite smitten with her. Of course, she could use all of this testimony in the courtroom, if it came to that, and she advised Miss Benedict to be ready for her cross-examination. The teacher agreed, and they left her to her duties.

Clara then traveled to Oakland to question the coroner, Travis Goodbody. She found the gentleman to be quite reticent about talking to her, but when she showed him her credentials as an attorney for George Kwong, the accused, he reluctantly agreed. When she asked him whether the mayor's office had contacted him about George Kwong and his internship, he said yes, He was, however, quite averse about talking further concerning the work the young man did or about the supposed theft of the post-mortem kit. Clara came away believing this man had been perhaps bribed or even threatened into cooperating with Bartlett.

She left the journalist, Stanley Boscombe, and the minister of the Tin How Joss House Temple, Guan Shi Yin, for last. In order to put her plan into effect, she left the same bit of information with each suspect. She told each person that when she went to trial to defend her client, George Kwong, she was going to surprise the jury with the identity of the killer. Clara then looked straight into the suspect's eyes and said, "I know it's you, and you should confess to me right now. Or else, your day of reckoning shall come in court." Of course, not one of the suspects confessed, but she was certain she had awakened the monster within, and that he or she would come after her.

As a matter of fact, Clara had no such incontrovertible evidence. She had suspicions, but she knew the only way to bring the killer out of hiding was to tell every suspect he or she was the murderer. Then, Clara was going to wait for this killer to come to her. The only person Clara had told about this spider-and-fly subterfuge was her good friend, Ah Toy. She believed if she told Captain Lees he would not allow her to do it, and nobody would catch this heinous killer. Ah Toy, on the other hand, was quite excited to hear about setting this trap. She was going to help her do it, and she suggested they discuss the details over a nice dinner at the Hopkins mansion on Nob Hill.

***

One Nob Hill, San Francisco, February 22, 1884

Later, inside the macabre Victorian mansion, Clara was dining with Ah Toy and Mrs. Hopkins. Ah Toy explained before dinner that the old woman was just about prepared to purchase some of Ah Toy's art. "She really wants my landscapes of Chinatown, and the ones I did of the Tin How Temple were especially pleasing to her. I'm afraid the old lady is going daft, however, and you must excuse her at dinner. Don't worry what you say because she will forget it in five minutes."

Clara realized this was true about Mrs. Mary Sherwood Hopkins when she told Ah Toy about her experience interviewing Stanley Boscombe and Guan Shi Yin. "When I told each one he was the killer and that he should confess to me right now, I got some rather interesting responses. The other suspects simply stated their innocence and some wanted to see my evidence. Mr. Boscombe, in a real panic, began to stutter profusely, and he eventually broke down in tears. The minister, on the other hand, began to pray in Cantonese. At least, that's what Ah Toy told me he was doing. His were the angriest prayers I have ever had the displeasure of hearing."

When both Clara and Ah Toy began to laugh at this, Mrs. Hopkins frowned. "You mustn't provoke God, my dear lady. Even the Chinese gods become belligerent." This made the levity even more boisterous, and soon Ah Toy and Clara were crying and laughing at the same time.

After they gained their composure, Clara explained how she was going to prepare herself for the probable attack by the killer. "After Captain Lees gave me the Derringer, I knew I had the responsibility to save the lives of women who might become targets of this killer's wrath. In addition, since the story of the killings has now circulated around the United States, I believe it will not infuriate this murderer, as the captain suggested. Instead, I think this killer will enjoy the notoriety such publicity will bring. Doesn't it stand to reason? Somebody who kills like this must be an extremely arrogant sort. This person must believe that he or she is doing society a favor by getting rid of these women."

"Yes, I saw a few of these types in my business as a Madame. They tend to be violent, and I had to restrict their access to my girls because it put them in danger of physical harm." Ah Toy nodded at the butler Hannigan who was bringing in a tray filled with the dinner's first course of mixed green salads.

"The mental state of the killer is a key to my

discovery of this person's identity. I believe that when I confronted him or her, I immediately caused fear to take hold. I suddenly became the person who must be killed next." Clara smiled up at Hannigan, who was placing the salad before her on the laced tablecloth. The butler did not return the smile, as he looked concerned about what she had just said.

"Don't you believe you might be in immediate danger? Perhaps you should seek protection." Ah Toy picked up her fork and held it aloft. "I know some Tongs who would do the job. Just give me your permission."

"No. That would scare off this perpetrator. In fact, it is my guess that I won't be approached until the trial. I told each suspect I was going to reveal the killer's identity during the trial, as a surprise. It would be reasonable to assume this megalomaniac, who may be testifying for the prosecution, will also bask in the limelight of such recognition, even though it is the light of truth." Clara picked up the canter of olive oil and spread it over her salad.

"The truth shall set you free!" exclaimed Mary Hopkins, between bites of her salad.

"I completely disagree! If this killer has any sanity left, he will attempt to kill you as soon as possible. The sooner you are out of the way, the sooner he can kill again." Ah Toy pointed her fork at Clara.

"No, this killer already knows he or she is a suspect. When I divulge the secret identity during the trial, it simply means I believe he or she is the real murderer. The authorities don't believe this, so the killer will simply declare his or her innocence in public, and then I shall truly be in danger of attack." Clara bit off a large piece of lettuce. "It is at that moment I may seek protection from your Tongs or from the police, if they'll give it to me."

"Hannigan! Get this poor woman some tongs. She can't pick up her salad!" Mrs. Hopkins cried.

***

As Clara walked to the streetcar after dinner, she began to feel the danger all around her. Why had she been so bold in her effort to bring this monstrous woman-killer out of hiding? She had five children and a family who depended on her. She wasn't a bachelor like Isaiah Lees. Perhaps her assessment of the murderer being arrogant was misplaced. It was she who was most arrogant. She believed her life was more important than those prostitutes and that the killer would treat her with respect. Why should the killer wait until the trial? Women were nothing to this person.

Clara saw that the slowly encroaching fog was making its way across the streets below Nob Hill. Clara clutched at her wrap, and pulled it down, so that it covered her top half. She had worn a thick cotton brown dress, with a large bustle, so her position while riding in the streetcar was uncomfortable. Her thoughts were even more discomforting, however. The man seated in the row across the aisle was staring at her. He was burly and red bearded, and he had a rather imposing dent in his forehead, as if someone had struck him with a hammer or other such tool. She wondered if her killer might not subcontract another murderer to get rid of her. That would be intelligent.

The fog was thick, as he followed her down Montgomery Street toward her apartment building. Clara heard the man's heavy steps. She smelled the foul odor from the man's cigar. As she increased her gait, he increased his, and her heart began to pound so forcefully that she felt its pulsing in her throat. She opened the top

95

two buttons on her dress. When she looked back, she saw nothing. The fog was too dense. She took a deep breath and began to run. She felt the bustle behind her swaying back and forth like a hot air balloon in the wind. Up ahead, as the fog began to clear, she saw the red awning in front of her building. She looked back, and the hammer head was still following her. She watched, as he began to run to catch up to her.

Was this going to be the moment of her demise? Could he be that mysterious dark figure she saw on the night of the McCarthy murder? Standing in the shadows with the flashing blade? No, she insisted upon living for her children. She extracted the Derringer from her purse and pointed it at the intruder. She felt the trigger on her finger, and her aim was steady. "Stop right there!"

The man raised his hands. "Whoa, Mrs. Foltz. I don't mean you no harm. Name's Sergeant O'Brien. Perry O'Brien. I work with Captain Lees. He wanted me to follow you." O'Brien held open his coat and showed her his SFPD badge.

Clara lowered the pistol to her side. "I am sorry, Detective. The captain didn't tell me he was ordering anybody to protect me. How long have you been following me?"

"All week. I guess when I was on the streetcar you were spooked by something. I've been tailing you so's you could question all your suspects without harm. And I'll be watching your apartment while you stay there. Officer Cameron will also wear plain clothes to switch with me so I can get some sleep." O'Brien took off his derby and held it in front of his portly stomach. Clara saw he was a redhead. "We'll be with you all next week during the trial. You can rest assured nobody will harm you as long as we're on the job, Mrs. Old Pinkerton'd have me head in a basket if you got harmed! Ever since the mayor fired him and his partner, Dutch Vanderheiden, he's vowed to help you defeat them in court."

Clara was astounded. "What did you say? Captain Lees lost his job because of me?"

"I don't think it was just you, Mrs. Clara. That old Englishman's been fighting Bartlett and his cronies in the Sheriff's Department for twenty years now. He says he's now going to do everything in his power to assist you."

Clara now knew that Isaiah Lees was truly a fine man. Unlike her ex-husband, who ran from any sign of conflict, and chased women like a barnyard rooster, this man Isaiah Lees was showing her his true mettle through his actions. She was probably more attracted to him now than she had ever before been lured by any man in her life.

"I must go in now, Mr. O'Brien. Please tell Captain Lees and his partner that I am indebted to them, and I'll certainly be making them members of my defense team."

"Yes, mum. I will certainly do that."

Clara climbed the front steps. When she turned around to see where he was, the detective tipped his derby toward her and grinned. "May those who love us, love us; and those who don't love us, may God turn their hearts; and if He don't turn their hearts, may he turn their ankles so we'll know them by their limping."

Clara turned the knob of the front door, and she felt truly safe for the first time that week.

Chapter Seven: The Trial

San Francisco City Hall Courthouse, San Francisco, February 23-27, 1884

O n the first day of the trial of George Kwong, there were thousands of demonstrators, mostly women, assembled outside the courthouse on Market and Van Ness Streets. Clara noticed that her friend from the Women's Suffrage Movement, Ellen Clark Sargent, was outside speaking to the assembled and handing out membership flyers. Clara often attended meetings of the Century Club at Ellen's home on Folsom Street.

The City Hall itself was a metaphor for public corruption. Its construction began in 1871, originally planned in the French-style, on the triangular space of the former Yerba Buena Park, which had previously been a cemetery. So many different contractors made a profit from the years of construction that they were fired, and others, even more corrupt, took their place.

The cheap, Greek-style structures that resulted had walls filled with sand, and the city hall buildings had two entrances, one of which faced North toward Van Ness and Nob Hill, where the wealthy could drive-up to the carriage entrance to do their business. The South-facing entrance to the city hall structures was where Clara and the demonstrators were. This was the Market Street side, which included the infamous "Sand Lots," where the labor unrest and Chinatown riots had begun.

As Clara passed by the suffragette group, on her way up the steps to the courthouse, Ellen Sargent waved. "You are our standard bearer, Clara Foltz! Portia of the Pacific, representing the rights of the underclasses, including women, is on her way to victory over the patriarchal powers. Just last year, this male-dominated system terminated the jobs of all the women inside San Francisco's City Hall and replaced them with men. Why? Not because the men were more competent at the jobs. No, they were replaced because men could vote. That's why we need to get that voting rights power, once and for all time!"

Inside the courtroom, the atmosphere and populace that made-up the ingredients of this so-called fair trial were diametrically opposed to the women outside demonstrating. As Clara had deduced earlier, Mayor Bartlett had hastily ordered a kangaroo court against her client, George Kwong.

She had only one week to prepare her case, and during that week she had to assess the tangible evidence, appear at the all-male Voir Dire jury rejection (she had to reject those jurists who were blatant racists), and bring George to the pre-trial hearing, where she argued for most of two hours, with Judge Randolph Hoffman, a man she had never before seen, to allow testimony from Chinese witnesses. She believed it was a pyrrhic victory when Hoffman permitted the testimony, because he warned her that her Asian witnesses could not be used as expert witnesses or eyewitnesses to a crime.

Now, as the trial docket was set, and she moved to

her defense table on the left side of the courtroom, she noticed with satisfaction that Captain Lees and Detective Vanderheiden were seated directly behind her and not on the prosecution's side of the room. Since they were no longer members of the police department, the two men would be testifying for her during the trial.

Ah Toy had been permitted to act as the court's translator and her personal legal assistant. Clara could smell the cigar and cigarette smoke coming from the visitors' gallery, and she smiled to herself when she realized that most of the visitors were male as well. The patriarchal hordes. Just the way she liked it.

Clara also had a secret plan she had executed before the witnesses were called to testify. She had told each one she believed he or she was the murderer and that she would surprise everyone during the trial with her announcement of who it was. Clara believed it would change everything. Even if this were a kangaroo trial, she would be able to flush out the real murderer from hiding. Ah Toy was the only other person who knew about her secret plan.

District Attorney Matthew C. Welles, Jr., was her adversary. He had a contingent of two other lawyers on his team of prosecutors, and they all dressed like pall bearers at a funeral. Black suits and ties, white shirts, and the collective demeanor of funeral directors. She assumed it was George Kwong's funeral they were going to prosecute.

"All rise!" the bailiff announced, standing next to the American flag. "The Honorable Randolph Charles Hoffman presiding in the case of the State of California versus George Bai Kwong, Docket number 53-C, Criminal Court, the State of California."

Clara felt a lump in her throat, as she always did

whenever she had to try a case. She had never graduated law school, and there was a voice inside that made her remember that fact. Even though she had made many male graduates look ridiculous, when she took the oral Bar Examination, as her photographic memory could recite most of the California Codes and Criminal Procedures verbatim.

Welles gave his opening statement to the 12 members of the jury. Unlike Clara, he was not a pacer. He spoke from his position of authority behind the prosecution's rostrum, but his voice was a deep baritone, and it was loud, so he need not visit each jurist the way Clara did when she addressed the panel.

"Gentlemen, I represent the people of the State of California. They have appointed me today to show you how the accused, George Kwong, was jilted by the victim, Miss Mary McCarthy, and in response, Kwong did knowingly and willfully attack her in the residence at 814 Sacramento Street at approximately seven in the evening of February 12, 1884."

Clara saw that Welles watched the faces of the jurymen very carefully. To her, they were the key to a successful argument.

"The State has a witness you will hear who will testify that George Kwong had a fight with the victim on the day before her murder, and another witness will explain how Kwong had learned to autopsy corpses while working as a coroner's assistant for a summer in Oakland. The victim, Miss McCarthy, who was trying to become an honest woman, was pulled back into prostitution by Kwong and his father, Andrew, who are well known to profit from such illegal enterprises in Chinatown."

The prosecutor's voice got noticeably louder. Clara

knew this was what men did when they wanted to get the upper hand with a woman in any argument.

"We will show that McCarthy was keeping money from such prostitution for herself, and that this enraged Kwong so much that he murdered her and stripped her corpse down to a mere skeleton, using the post-mortem kit he obtained from his job in Oakland. Kwong wanted to make Miss McCarthy an example to other women who would attempt such independence in the future."

There were several gasps and groans from jury members during his speech and a few shouts from the audience.

"We shall also show that this planning against independent prostitutes was well known by the police, especially the Chinatown Squad, and that the Kwongs kept a strict business practice and detested any such absconding of money by women like Miss McCarthy. In fact, their Tong enforcers, the San Ho Jui, or Triad Society, made certain these women were kept in line and paid the Kwongs regularly for their work in the flesh trade."

Again, there were audible gasps from the gallery. Clara noticed that several of the jury members were getting red in the face and fidgeting in their seats. Not a good sign.

"We know this murder can be the tip of an iceberg of corruption in Chinatown, and these criminals, left unchecked, will continue to import and kidnap innocent women to continue their business. Miss McCarthy's murder is perhaps the beginning of a widespread conspiracy to plant terror in the minds of women who would think about going against the dictates of the criminal element in Chinatown. Mr. George Kwong, who is guilty of enforcing the will of his elders, must pay for his criminal act, and we are here to prove his murderous guilt beyond any reasonable man's doubt."

Several men in the gallery applauded, and one even whistled, until the judge finally struck his gavel to restore order.

Judge Hoffman turned to Clara. "Thank you, Counselor. Mrs. Foltz? Would you like to give your opening statement?"

Clara rose from her chair, spread out the front of her conservative, dark-blue dress with the medium-sized bustle in the rear, and walked over to stand in front of the jury. She hoped the intelligent logic of her words could overcome her obvious lack of audible force.

"Shall we get the rather obvious facts out of the way first, gentlemen? I am a female representing another minority, a Chinese man by the name of George Kwong. I have no obligation by law to prove that Mr. Kwong did not commit this heinous murder. No, the only requirement to defend him, since he is not guilty in the eyes of the law up until that moment when Mr. Welles proves his accusations to you, is to show you the number of ways my client may have not reasonably committed the act in question. This horrible act was done to a woman, Miss Mary McCarthy, who was in love with my client, and he was in love with her."

A few men in the audience laughed. Clara began to pace, moving from one juror to the next and looking each in the eye.

"In fact, the defense will show through testimony and evidence that George was attempting to get her out of her sinful profession and not into it, as the prosecution alleges. I will not argue that Andrew Kwong is innocent of taking money from the Tongs, who run the prostitution and other illicit enterprises inside Chinatown. Instead, I will show how these illicit businesses have come about because of many years of racism and restriction of basic human rights."

When several in the audience booed, Clara felt the obvious prejudice for the first time in that courtroom. She did not look their way, however. Instead, she increased the volume of her voice to its maximum.

"The Chinese in San Francisco came to our city with the hope of eventually becoming citizens. However, their overlords in southern China, the Manchu, and their overlords in this country, the owners of the railroads, conspired together to prevent these innocent workers from gaining any civil rights in these United States. Instead, they were attacked and some were murdered by mobs. They were not allowed outside of their ghettos to mingle with their fellow workers and citizens, and they needed protection just to exist."

Again, there were shouts and cat-calls. Judge Hoffman finally struck his gavel several times to quiet the rowdy crowd.

"The Tongs became that protection, and they were often independent from the Six Companies because they threatened decent men like the Kwongs with violence if they did not submit. Did the authorities help them gain respect and citizenship? No, instead, they appointed a special Chinatown Squad to harass and to subject them to demeaning searches and, in some cases, even killing babies with deadly fumigants and sprays."

Several of the jury members said "No!" Others frowned and coughed.

"Counselor Foltz. Please stay on the topic of murder in the first degree." Judge Hoffman admonished her by striking his gavel.

"It's all related, your honor. The Kwongs were two men who worked the most to show they were part of our community. Andrew learned to speak fluent English, and he even converted from his natural-born faith to become a Methodist. His son, George, worked with him on the only permitted newspaper, *The Oriental*, so they could spread the good, Christian news of redemption and hope to his fellow Chinese. These were not men who detested our culture. These were men who loved our city and our citizens."

Two Chinese men in the back row cheered. They were Clara's permitted witnesses, and the judge immediately said, "Silence! Or I shall have you both thrown out of my court!"

Clara, unbowed, continued, "Why would my client want to jeopardize his future by killing a white woman? We women have so few rights as it is. Why would a good, upstanding Chinese man want to kill the woman he loved and to whom he had devoted his time in order to save her from the world's oldest profession? This is a profession, gentlemen, which women have been forced to enter, when their rights were violated, when men have raped them, and then they have gone unpunished."

Clara noticed, as she began moving from one juror to the next, that her words were having an effect. Their faces softened, and several of them were actually nodding their heads in agreement.

"George Kwong wanted to save his lover, Mary McCarthy, not kill her. Love does not kill. Love preserves. It preserves our human dignity, and it returns our basic human rights to us if we earn them, just as the Kwongs have earned them. Thank you, kind gentlemen of the jury."

"Mr. Welles, you may call your first witness," Judge Hoffman pointed to the bailiff to swear in the summoned person by the witness stand.

"Your honor, I call Stanley Boscombe to the stand."

The young journalist from the *San Francisco Examiner* walked over to stand before the uniformed bailiff. "Please raise your right hand, and place your left hand on the Bible," the bailiff instructed. Boscombe, as well as all the other witnesses that day, did so. "Do you solemnly swear, to tell the truth, the whole truth and nothing but the truth, so help you God?"

"I do," Boscombe said.

"You may be seated," the bailiff said.

Stanley Boscombe sat down in the witness chair next to the judge's raised platform. Clara cross-examined three witnesses that day. Boscombe, whom the prosecution attempted to use as a witness to George Kwong's being present before the murder took place, was rebutted by asking him questions about the purpose of journalism.

"Isn't it the job of a journalist to be on the scene of a crime in order to transcribe what occurred? Could my client have been there to take a photograph of the crime scene? Did George Kwong have a weapon on him?"

These interrogatives were all answered in the affirmative, except the last, which was a "no." Clara knew it was her purpose to put a reasonable doubt in the minds of the jurors, nothing else, and this was what she did.

The second witness for the prosecution was Rachel Benedict, the teacher at the Methodist Home for Wayward Women in Chinatown. She was on Clara's list of prime suspects, even though Clara doubted that she had performed the actual murders. Captain Lees explained that the strength required to flay a woman the way those victims had been dissected, most definitely required the force of a man. Of course, Benedict could still be guilty as an accessory.

Welles's line of questioning attempted to prove that the personal relations between George Kwong and Mary McCarthy had been toxic and that when George left the mission that day before the murder, he was especially angry at McCarthy.

Clara cross-examined Benedict by asking pointed yes-or-no questions. Did the defendant bring Mary McCarthy to you for help? Did the defendant help you by giving money to the home? Did you see George Kwong and Mary McCarthy enjoying themselves? Did the argument you witnessed escalate into anything physical? All of these answers, except the last one, were answered affirmatively, and Clara believed she had planted her seeds of doubt in the minds of the jurors.

The final witness for the prosecution that day was the coroner from Oakland, Travis Goodbody. As predicted, Goodbody was asked to identify George Kwong as the man he employed for the summer internship. The second attorney on the prosecution's team, William Varson, did the questioning of this key witness. Varson had a habit of looking back at the judge after every question, as if he were pleading to God. Clara, on the other hand, always gave her reiterations of witness responses directly to the jury. The jury, after all, decided the guilt or innocence of her client.

Varson continued with his examination of the coroner by bringing forth the Civil War post-mortem kit, the alleged tools used to strip the flesh and hone the body of the victim. Varson asked several highly technical questions about how this process could be accomplished on a female body, and Goodbody swore that these tools could do the job. Clara objected when Varson tried to ask whether George Kwong asked Goodbody any questions relating to using any of the tools to kill someone, and the judge, thankfully, sustained her demurrer, and struck the question from the record.

Clara had her own rebuttal witness, whom she would be presenting after the prosecution was finished with its witnesses, and she smiled over at him after she asked Goodbody her only cross-examination question.

"Do you keep your tools under lock and key?" she asked.

"No," Goodbody said. Clara turned around and grinned at Lees, and he smiled back.

***

Later that evening, Ah Toy told Clara she believed the first day had gone well, especially Clara's brilliant opening statement. The defense team, composed of Clara, Ah Toy, Captain Lees and his partner, Dutch Vandenheiden, were dining together at the Luck Dragon in Chinatown. The large restaurant was filled with many of the visiting female demonstrators from across the United States, and Clara was somewhat of a celebrity to them.

The owner, Stephen Fong of the Hip Kat Company, was personally seeing to it that Clara and her party were given the royal treatment. The table was filled with the most delectable and freshest dishes, and their teapot was refilled regularly during the meal.

"It all seems so choreographed and ritualized. I keep thinking I'm simply talking to walls with animal trophy heads on them. Don't you agree, Isaiah? This is just a kangaroo trial." Clara sipped from her small teacup, and then wiped her lips with a cloth napkin.

"What do you have planned, Clara? You knew this would happen going in because I told you as much. Despite your newspaper victory, and all these demonstrators, the country is still against the Chinese. The economy's been hemorrhaging jobs like blood oozing out of one of this killer's victims, and the Chinese are seen as threats to the few remaining jobs for men." Captain Lees picked up a fried wonton and began to chew it.

Clara looked over at Ah Toy. "Shall I tell them?"

Ah Toy nodded. "I think you need to at this point."

"You never told me you would have one of your men, a Detective O'Brien, I think his name is, following me around day and night. Well, I never told you that I have a plan to bring the real killer out of hiding." Clara stabbed one of her chopsticks into a bowl of fried rice. "I informed every suspect on our list that he or she was the murderer. I also told him or her I was going to prove it as a surprise during the trial."

Lees pounded his fist on the table. "You did what? Are you insane?"

"Now wait a minute, boss. Why would telling them they're guilty do anything to bring them out? Why would they risk killing Clara until they knew what she had on them?" Vanderheiden said, twirling the end of his auburn mustache.

"What do you have on this *real* killer? Who is it?" Lees scowled at her.

Clara looked down at her hands. She felt the same way she had when she lied to her father while she was secretly meeting Jeremiah Foltz. She looked back up and confronted Isaiah's dark eyes. Her fear of real commitment with a man was still plaguing her. "I don't have anything, really. I need to prove a few things first. I

109

just thought since this was a kangaroo court anyway, I would just …"

"Just commit suicide?" Lees roared.

"If the killer tries to get me, then I shall perhaps save some other poor woman. I promise. I won't accuse anyone during the trial. I simply thought my ruse would flush out the killer. Besides, you gave me the gun." Clara's voice dropped to a whisper.

"I gave you that gun to give you confidence, not real protection. This killer obviously means business. I wouldn't doubt he knows how to wear chest armor or even something like a knight's helmet. We had robbers in England who did this whilst terrorizing a bank. Your Derringer's bullets would be like hitting the killer with two beanbags."

"I agree with Detective Vanderheiden," Ah Toy said. "This murderer won't risk killing a famous person like Clara. Not unless Clara named that person in court and proved why he or she is guilty." Ah Toy took Clara's hands into her own and engaged her eyes. "Since you won't be showing anything like that during the trial, then there is no danger."

"What do you think is our best way to proceed? I am going to put you on the stand, Isaiah, and the questions I will ask are going to relate to the way this city has its hands in corrupt activities." Clara stared hard at the Captain of Detectives. Even though she had known him just a brief time, she cared about him.

"I can only tell the truth. If my superiors can't handle the truth, then getting my job back isn't worth my time and effort. I've already told you a lot of what you used in your opening statement today. Also, when you wrote that editorial about how the Chinese are being treated, I was completely supportive. I do agree with you about this being the only way to fight this accusation against your client. Without you, Clara, George Kwong would already be hanging from Russian Hill." Lees grasped Clara's hands and scowled.

"All right then. We will attempt to put the mayor and the Chinatown Squad on trial, if that's the only way I can fight. I need to get some sleep now, so I bid you all adieu, my friends. Thank you for your cooperation."

Clara stood up, arranged her hat, and buttoned the top button at her throat. "Once more, into the fray!"

***

The next day in court, the prosecution finished its presentation of evidence and witnesses. Sheriff Connolly, the arresting officer, testified that his men found the post-mortem kit under George Kwong's mattress, and when asked about it, the Defendant had told him he did not know how it got there. Clara was able to get Connolly to admit that anybody with access to the house could have placed the kit under the mattress.

She also pointed out the fact that as the Coroner for the City of Oakland, Travis Goodbody was also affiliated with the police department. She asked Connolly if police did favors for each other in order to get a conviction, and the sheriff admitted that "in order to make the law run smoothly, its officers needed to cooperate to convict a murderer."

Welles and his prosecution team spent the rest of the day presenting detailed charts and statistics that claimed to show how Chinatown profited from its prostitution businesses. When Welles said that it was "common knowledge" that when a woman became independent, she was a direct threat to the profits made by the Six

Companies, especially Andrew Kwong and his family, Clara objected.

She explained to the judge that this was hearsay, and without specific contracts or testimony proving that the Kwongs profited directly from Chinatown prostitution, it was inadmissible. Sadly, Judge Hoffman overruled her, and permitted the accusations and statistical information.

Clara spent that night coaching both Captain Lees and her assistant, Ah Toy. They were going to be the first two witnesses she was going to call. She first spent a half hour at the Luck Dragon talking with two journalists from the East Coast who were covering the trial for their newspapers.

One, a gentleman from the *New York Times*, seemed more interested in the fact she was the first woman lawyer in California than he did about the case itself and what it represented. The second, a woman, who was writing for the private newspaper of the Women's Suffrage Movement under Susan B. Anthony, was more sympathetic to the plight of Clara attempting to get a fair trial under such patriarchal hegemony.

After they left, Clara went over what she was going to try to do with her questions the next day in court. "I want to show how the Chinatown Squad was formed, and I want to show how it has treated the Chinese unfairly from its inception. Also, I want to prove that independent prostitution has been permitted in the past, and that women like you, Ah Toy, have actually made a success of it under dire circumstances."

"I think you should talk about the so-called post-mortem kit again," Lees pointed out. "Those tools are too small and flimsy to be used to slice through thick muscle and sinew. When Dutch and I found the body, our first thought was that a Tong member had done the work because they use these large hatchet-like knives that would be ideal for this kind of hideous flaying of a human body."

"Good thinking, Isaiah," Clara said. "I thought those tools looked small. After all, they are meant to be used on the battlefield during the war, as anything larger would have been cumbersome."

"I'll tell you anything you need to relate about the business, Clara, you know that. Besides, if Mrs. Hopkins found out I was in the news she would find it humorous. The first thing she told me when she found out I had been a Madame was that husbands should pay their wives more for that activity. If they did, then maybe the husbands wouldn't have to frequent bordellos so often."

It rained all the next day, and during Clara's questioning, there were flashes of lightning and bursts of thunder. It was as if the gods were taking her to task for the information she was spreading about the corruption of police in San Francisco.

She was objected to five times by the prosecution, but she knew her witnesses had already responded, so the jury was able to hear his testimony nevertheless. It was a trick her lawyer father taught her about being a lawyer. "The horse is already out of the barn," was the way he put it to her.

When she called Captain Isaiah Lees to the stand, there was a hushed stillness inside the courtroom. The newspapers had already informed the city about Lees being fired by Mayor Bartlett, and the story about why the Captain of Detectives had turned against the mayor was also covered. Many people believed Lees was justified for becoming a witness for the defense, but most thought he was a traitor.

Clara, however, knew that the entire hope of freeing her client in that court rested on the captain's testimony. She walked slowly up to him on the witness stand and looked him straight in the eyes.

"How long have you been working for the San Francisco Police Department, Captain Lees?" Clara asked.

"Twenty-three years, six months and fifteen days," Lees replied.

"What reason did the authorities give for your sudden termination on February 22, of this year?"

"I was told I had assisted you, the defense, in this case and that it was against police department regulations to do so." Clara saw Isaiah's forehead begin to sweat, as he was obviously under a lot of pressure.

"Is it true, Captain Lees, that you are required by law to hand over to the defense all evidence and lists of witnesses that will be called by the prosecution before the trial begins?"

"Yes, that's very true. I have often even worked with the defense to make certain they have all of this information or else a mistrial could be ordered by the court."

"I object, your honor! Counsel knows full well that handing over relevant evidence and a list on a piece of paper must first go through the judge's hands. Captain Lees never did this. He is therefore in violation of police department policy." Welles was livid.

"Objection sustained." Judge Hoffman ordered.

Clara decided to get into her main questions.

"Captain, were you working for the San Francisco Police Department when the Chinatown Squad was formed?"

"Yes, I certainly was. The formation of the

Chinatown Squad came shortly after the passage of the federal Chinese Exclusion Law by Congress in 1882."

"In your expert opinion, Captain, do you believe this sheriff's department sub-group was acting in the best interests of justice?" Clara rubbed her forehead. "Can you tell the court of any examples of a direct miscarriage of justice caused by this organization?"

"Again, objection! What does this have to do with the first degree murder of Mary McCarthy?"

The judge thought for a moment. Finally, he said, "Objection overruled. This pressure on the Chinese population is relevant to the mental state of the defendant."

"Thank you, your honor. And so, Captain Lees? What happened to cause you to turn against the Chinatown Squad?" Clara looked over at the jury to be certain they were listening. They were.

"I saw a Chinese baby killed from the fumigation by Jesse Brown Cook of the Chinatown Squad."

Several people shouted. There were gasps and jeers.

"The Sheriff blamed every outbreak of disease on the Chinese," Lees continued. "The Chinatown Squad was often more of a hindrance to crime fighting than it was an aide. I also saw men who took money from public officials in order to put more pressure on the Chinese men working in Chinatown."

"Thank you, Captain Lees. And now, what about the so-called murder weapon? The Civil War field autopsy kit that my client, George Kwong, supposedly used on the victims? In your considered opinion, could these tools have been used successfully to accomplish this dastardly and horrendous deed?"

"Objection. Witness is not an authority." Welles shouted.

"The witness was in the army during the Civil War, your honor," Clara said.

"Objection overruled. You may respond, Captain Lees," Hoffman said.

"Let me see that kit. I'll show you why it could never have been used to do the job on the victim," Lees said.

The field kit was carried over to Lees by the bailiff. The captain pulled out the largest scalpel from the kit, which was about six inches long, and held it up for the jury to see. "Mrs. Foltz. Could you assist me for a moment and come over here?"

Clara, who had rehearsed this earlier, dramatically approached the witness stand and held out her arm to Lees. The captain asked her roll up her dress sleeve, which she did. He then held the small, silver blade against the thick part of her forearm.

"This blade could have never been large enough to cut through the sinew of a woman's forearm, much less eviscerate her and slice through the thick muscles of the biceps and the thighs. Even if razor-sharp, it would have taken so much time to accomplish this feat that the murderer would have certainly been discovered." Lees brushed the small blade lightly against Clara's white skin, and again the gallery shouted its displeasure.

"This kit was made for emergencies on the battle field, was it not, Captain? But, what about a Tong hatchet? Could this have accomplished the murderous intent of the killer? Please, Mr. Andrew Kwong. Can you bring over one of your Tong hatchets for the jury to see?" Clara called out to the father, who was seated in the front row on the defense side.

After Andrew Kwong held the large, sixteen-inch

blade with an oak handle up, the courtroom again began to shout and whistle.

"Order! I shall have this court cleared if I hear any more commotion!" Judge Hoffman said, slamming his gavel down repeatedly.

"That is all, Captain. I thank you. I wish to call Miss Ah Toy to the stand, your honor." Clara winked at Isaiah, and he smiled back at her as he left the witness stand.

After she was sworn in, Ah Toy took a seat on the stand. She seemed very poised in her red silk *cheongsam*, and she looked over at the men in the jury box. They were all staring at her.

"Miss Ah Toy. At one time, you were working as an independent Madame in Chinatown, were you not?" Clara wanted to establish her witness's professional status.

"Yes, I was. I worked for fifteen years in that capacity."

"Could you show the court why your independent status was superior to the methods of prostitution provided by the Tongs and their sex slavery work conditions?"

"I would be very happy to do that," said Ah Toy, and she stood up. When both of her arms began to undulate in the air, like weaving cobras, the jury panel became transfixed. Clara could see their eyes bulge as they stared at Ah Toy. She then began to wave her bottom in a circular fashion, so the outline of her firm buttocks could be seen clearly under the soft silk.

It took five minutes before Judge Hoffman could become rational. "That's enough! The witness will be seated at once!"

"Your honor, what does this prove?" whined Prosecutor Welles.

"Counselor Foltz?" the judge inquired.

"Miss Ah Toy, were you demonstrating the main method of your female allure that you taught to all of your prostitutes? Were they paid well, were they healthy, and did you even allow some to marry if they so chose?"

"Yes to all of your questions. I made most of my money without having my women engage in any intercourse with their patrons." Ah Toy's voice was clear and confident.

"And, what about the Tong's method?" Clara asked, turning to the jury.

"The Tongs bought and sold their women like sex slaves. They were kept in wire cages, and all of them had to have intercourse or be sent back to China. Profit was the main goal of the Tong method." Ah Toy raised her fist in the air. "Never again should this be allowed!"

The courtroom erupted in a mixture of shouts, cheers, and jeers. Judge Hoffman had to adjourn to prevent a riot.

***

The final day, Clara brought to the stand her Chinese contingent of witnesses. With Ah Toy acting as translator, she questioned the head of the San Ho Hui, Xi Ming, who testified that he often paid bribes to various police officials so as to keep them from arresting his women. Welles objected that Ming was "no expert witness," and the judge sustained his objection. Clara also interviewed Andrew Kwong at length to explain the good deeds he did for his community and for the Methodist Church and its outreach. He also testified about his son, George, and that he had never had any discipline problems from him at all. Clara interviewed the minister of the Tin How Temple, Guan Shi Yin, who stated that the defendant George Bai Kwong had helped him with religious services

118

and ceremonial duties.

Finally, Clara questioned a Chinese prostitute who knew George. She stated that George was always trying to get women out of the profession and into a "respectable line of work." She also said she knew that was what he was doing with Mary McCarthy.

When instructed by Judge Hoffman to present their final summations, Welles did not speak. He had brought in a special closing argument specialist, one Harold Rossiter, a Sacramento District Attorney. Rossiter, unlike the "pallbearer" Welles, spoke to each of the male jurors individually. His most passionate and affective speech came when he was discussing the threat of violence and disease on womanhood.

"If you allow this man to go free, what are you telling our Christian women in San Francisco? That you care nothing about their lives? For, make no mistake, gentlemen. This killer will strike again. He has already chosen a white woman, and who will be the next victim? It could be your wife, sir, or yours, sir! The bloody handwriting is on the walls of Chinatown's opium dens and inside its brothels. Unless you put a stop to it, it will become an infestation of gruesome murders, and the blood will be on your hands, Gentlemen, unless you vote today for a conviction of murder in the first degree!"

In her closing statement, Clara thought she was not going to do it, but she did. She mentioned the seven Chinese prostitutes who had been killed.

"I know you swore that you never read anything about this case before becoming a jurist. I must say that is how our system works best. Jurors must not be emotionally swayed by members of the press before or during a trial. That is why we have jury sequestration."

Clara moved again in front of each juror as she spoke. There eyes were a bit glassy, so she decided to get into the main thrust of her argument.

"I must tell you that there have been women murdered before Miss McCarthy, gentlemen of the jury. But they were Chinese women, and they were also independent women, trying to be like my witness Ah Toy. They simply wanted to be able to work their way out of this life of sin and brutality in order to see another day of hope. But, they were struck down in their youth, just like the victim in this case."

Clara strutted over to stand before her client, George Kwong. "George Kwong, my client, had no reason to commit this act of brutality. He wanted to save women like her from this life. He could not save the seven others of his own race, and he could not save the life of the one woman with whom he fell in love."

Seeing that the jury members' eyes were again riveted on her, she swayed her bustle a bit to draw their attention even more.

"The weapon was not seen in his hand, the testimony of his anger at Mary McCarthy is mixed, at best, and the fact that he worked one summer as a coroner's apprentice speaks to the fact that my client wanted to learn another trade besides journalism. He was not planning to kill anybody, and he just wanted what his father, Andrew, was attempting to get. Respect as a citizen of San Francisco, who wanted to become a United States citizen one day and sit with you outside the ghetto of Chinatown. You must acquit my client today, gentlemen, for the good of humanity and for the best interests of justice."

Having completed her summary, Clara walked over to her table and sat down. She took George Kwong's hands into her own, and she shed tears. He smiled back at her and whispered, "Thank you."

***

It took only six hours for the jury to deliberate. When they filed back into the courtroom, Clara and Ah Toy had returned from lunch. They stood at their positions at the Defense table. Clara kept staring at the American flag as Judge Hoffman requested the verdict from the jury foreman. The foreman, a short man with a brush mustache, looked tired.

"Has the jury reached a verdict in the case of the State of California versus George Bai Kwong?" Judge Hoffman asked.

"Yes, we have, Your Honor. We find the defendant guilty of first degree murder."

There were shouts and flashes from dozens of cameras inside the courtroom. Outside, there were protesting screams from the demonstrators.

Clara and Ah Toy refused to talk to any journalists. Clara put her arm around George Kwong, who was crying unabashedly. She leaned over and whispered, "It's not over yet. I believe I know who the killer is."

Chapter Eight: The Kidnapping and Trap

One Nob Hill, Hopkins Mansion, San Francisco, February 28, 1884

Clara, Ah Toy, Andrew Kwong, Isaiah Lees, and Eduard Vanderheiden sat around the large, rosewood table inside Ah Toy's bedroom. Since her bedroom in the Hopkins mansion was larger than most living rooms in other houses, the group had more than enough room to discuss the case and plan their next move. Both Clara and Captain Lees foresaw what the result was to be, and thus they knew there must be an alternative to allowing George Kwong to swing from a rope.

After praising Clara and Ah Toy for the job they did at the trial, Lees became his usual, somber self. "I have fought the public hangings in San Francisco from the start. If you have never seen one of these events, then you have not seen the lowest state to which humanity can be reduced. I have seen men foul themselves, cry like babies, trip, curse, hang without dying for over ten minutes, snap the rope, and laugh at it all in a delusional madness. Meanwhile, the authorities, including the conservative merchants of San Francisco, reap great profits from the sinful spectacle. I will not allow it to happen again!"

Andrew Kwong made a karate chop in the air. "I am

with you, Captain! What do you suggest we do?"

"I've thought about this long and hard. When your son was first arrested, I knew the White Whale, Washington Bartlett, would never allow George to have a fair trial. Therefore, the only way to save him from Russian Hill is to kidnap him from the jail on Kearny." The scowl of concentration had returned to Lees' face. "And we can bring him here for safekeeping until we can track down the real killer."

"Do you believe me?" Clara took Lees' hand. "I promise you, Isaiah. I know who the murderer is. However, if I give the identity of this monster, I know you will make an arrest. After this trial, I now realize the evidence I have will not be sufficient for the State to convict. The only way I can make the arrest, and perhaps expose any collaborators, will be to lure the murderer to us. And you must promise not to force me to tell you who I suspect until this person is captured."

Captain Lees frowned. "I reluctantly agree. However, if I were still on the force, I would not have agreed. You understand that my first concern is human life?"

"Yes. I understand. However, I must lure this killer out of his or her lair. I can't tell you any more than that."

"Carrie, I knew you had an answer! How will you get the killer here?" Ah Toy used the familiar name for her friend, knowing this was an important moment.

"Carrie? I've never heard you called that," Lees said.

"My parents gave it to me at birth. I changed it later to a more officious title. I believe this killer has an obsession about independent women. Although I don't know what is in this sick person's mind, I do know that if we can escalate the independent threat, then this person

123

will become so enraged that he or she will attempt to come here in order to murder again."

Clara unfastened the top button on her dress and took a deep breath. "Once again, I plan to use the power of the press to arouse the passions of this killer. What if Ah Toy shows women how to use their feminine magnetism to make money from men? We can then advertise a course to teach women these skills. We can say that each course enrollee will have a private meeting with her, beforehand, in this mansion, in order to ascertain the specific needs of the student."

"Yes! That private meeting will tell the killer it will be an excellent way to eliminate me." Ah Toy's face radiated with inner excitement at the prospect of danger.

"I won't be able to guarantee at which appointment the killer will appear, as I would assume he or she would not use his or her real name or true gender. Therefore, I will have to be ready to protect you at every such rendezvous inside the mansion." Clara took Ah Toy's hands in her own. "You are so very brave to be doing this."

"Not only will I be assisting you in trapping this murderer, I will also be preparing the lessons needed to educate a new generation of women who want to gain independence and profit from the male patriarchy." Ah Toy smiled. "I would assume these two powerful men will be helping us in our trap. And, if you need more assistance, I do know some Tong men who would be more than willing to pitch-in."

Dutch Vanderheiden snorted. "Say what? No Tongs allowed. If Mayor Bartlett or any of his henchmen saw even one Chinaman around this place, they'd raid us in a heartbeat. Just keeping Georgie boy inside will be difficult enough."

"Where can we stash the boy so nobody will see him?" Captain Lees liked to get everything prepared before he did anything. "It should preferably be somewhere nobody would wander into by accident."

"There's an observatory in the largest steeple. It's a small room, but it is out of way, and George will be comfortable," Ah Toy said.

"Fine. Show us where it is before we go. I want to be able to enter and go directly up there. The faster we can lock him away, the better." Lees stood up and motioned for his partner. "We need to go now, Dutch. We have to plan our kidnapping adventure before we arrive. It won't be easy, but those oafs in the sheriff's jail can be tricked if we do things correctly."

"Right, boss, we can do it. They don't call you Pinkerton around the station for nothing." Dutch followed the shorter man to the door. Ah Toy minced her way over to the door and opened it.

"Lead on, Ah Toy. Clara, you can start drafting your advertisement for the newspapers, and after we return with George Kwong, you can begin your part of this endeavor."

"Good luck, Isaiah and Eduard. I am so grateful to you both. You're putting your careers and possibly your lives at risk," Clara said, smiling at them.

The observatory was a good hiding place. It was up a long, winding stairway, and the room was very dark and sinister, with a skylight that looked out at the stars above San Francisco. A small bed, a lamp, a chair, and a telescope for viewing the sky. Lees and Dutch thanked Ah Toy and left.

***

It was a long walk from Nob Hill to the jail on Kearny, so Lees and Vanderheiden took the cable car. They

125

discussed how they would break George Kwong out the same way they discussed all their cases together. Lees began by laying out the plan, and Dutch filled in the details.

"Smith knows me, so we can work on him. I've been on hanging details before, so I know the protocol. The prisoner always has to see the doctor before he can be hanged. That always made me scratch my head. Why does the poor bastard have to be healthy to get his neck broken? Because it's the law." Lees took out his Bowie knife from his vest and began to clean under his fingernails. An elderly couple seated in the opposite row gave him a fearful look. Captain Lees just smiled at them.

Lees continued, "We can tell Smith we need to take Kwong to Doc Reed around the corner on Market. I'll tell Smith that Doc Reed gave us permission to escort the prisoner to him. We still have our weapon permits. We need the extra money since we're no longer working."

"But they'll know we were the last officers to be seen with him. What about that?" Dutch stretched his long legs under the seat in front of him.

"We both run like three-toed sloths. We'll just say the kid broke away from us and ran like a deer. We lost him in the crowds of all those women suffragettes. Couldn't shoot because we didn't want to hit a tourist." Lees finished his nails and slid the knife back into its leather sheath under his cape.

"Right. Ha! All those screaming women got us bamboozled." Dutch laughed.

"You take Kwong to the mansion, and I'll go back and tell Smith what happened. I'll say you're still out there hunting for the escaped prisoner, and I just wanted to get word out for a dragnet to begin. You know Connolly will call out the cavalry on this one. The White Whale will swallow him whole if he doesn't." Lees stood up, as they had arrived at their stop.

As they strolled together toward the jail, Dutch began a discussion about Clara Foltz. It had been bothering him from the moment his boss decided to take sides in the trial of George Kwong. Lees had always been somewhat sympathetic to the Chinese immigrants, but it was only based on the fact he was also an immigrant, and his boss's job went more smoothly when Lees treated the Chinese with respect. With Foltz, however, there had been an obvious change in Lees' entire demeanor and purpose.

Dutch took out a cigar from his frock coat pocket, bit off the end, spat out the piece into the gutter, and plugged the cigar between his teeth. He grimaced, took a box of wooden matches from the same pocket, slid the drawer open, took out a single match, and struck it against a lamp post on the sidewalk. He brought the blazing match to the end of the cigar and puffed. Plumes of smoke arose all around him as he walked.

"You really enjoy the company of Mrs. Foltz. I never seen you so attracted to a woman before, boss. Why her?"

"I don't really understand it myself," Lees said, rubbing his goatee. "I suppose she's the first woman I've ever met who has both brains and beauty. Also, she defends her family the way my own mother did. My mother never gave me heartache when I came to this country. She knew it was hard in England for me, and she understood my itch for adventure. That's just the way Clara strikes me. She appreciates an adventurous heart, but she defends the hearth and home."

"I see. I won't be asking again," Dutch said, puffing

on his stogie as they came up to the station house on Kearny.

Lees walked up the steps and waved to his partner. "I'll meet you back out here," he said, pushing open the door with his shoulder.

"Okay, boss. Give 'em hell." Dutch turned around and walked to the corner near a lamppost, still puffing on his cigar.

Sergeant Smith greeted Lees. "Pinkerton, where's Dutch? In the gin mill, as usual?"

"Sergeant, your perception decries the intelligence of your station. I'm here to transport Kwong over to Doctor Reed for his check-up. Dutch is outside. Doc Reed gave us this special detail because we're out of work now. Can you bring him down for me, oh inspirational one?" Lees joked, hoping to keep up his casual appearance.

"Right, Captain. I am sorry about your run-in with Connolly and those sheriff bastards. They've been a thorn in our hide for many years."

Smith turned around and shouted up the stairs, "Goose! Bring down the dead chink. Captain's taking him to Doc Reed."

"The man deserves to be called by his given name, Sergeant. And, as far as I know, he's still on this Earth." Lees admonished.

"Anything you say, Captain." Smith returned to his desk.

Ten minutes later, Lees greeted the prisoner, who was in shackles around his wrists and his ankles. "Mr. Goose, is it? We won't be needing those chains. Unlock him. I take full responsibility."

"O'Hara, Captain," the officer said, and he looked over at Sergeant Smith. Smith nodded, and O'Hara took a key from his belt and unlocked first the wrist chain, and then bent down and unlocked the ankle chain. "You be a good boy for the Captain, now George," he said.

Outside, on the sidewalk, Dutch was waiting for his boss and Kwong, smoking the rest of his cigar. When they walked up, he flipped the butt into the gutter. "Did Smith question your motives, boss?"

"No, he was his irritable self, but he was cooperative. We need to take Kwong down this alleyway to go to Chinatown. We can't trust the main thoroughfare." Lees took George Kwong's arm and guided him toward the alley entrance. Dutch followed them.

They were almost at Portsmouth Square when Lees stopped. "I will now go back and report to the station about the escape. You take Kwong over to Nob Hill, but go by the side streets and not up California Street."

"Where will I meet you?" Vanderheiden looked around in the shadows of the alley. He heard footsteps, coming fast and hard. Before he could get his gun out of his holster, he was tackled by a large man and held to the ground, with his arms twisted behind his back.

Lees, however, had seen the attack coming much sooner, and his .45 was drawn and pointed at the man holding his partner face-down in the dirty puddles of the alley.

"Captain! Behind you!" George Kwong shouted.

Lees spun around, slipping his Bowie knife from its sheath in the same motion. The Tong gang member screamed something in Chinese as the six-inch hatchet in his hand came up toward the captain's throat, in an attempt to decapitate him.

In a dexterous move for his fifty-four years, Lees dropped down, and he could hear the blade pass over his head. He struck with his own knife, slicing behind the attacker's legs, cutting into his Achilles tendons in two quick strokes. The gang member fell to his knees, screaming what Lees assumed to be curses, and grabbed at his ankles, which were now bleeding profusely.

Pointing his gun at the other attacker, Lees told George, "Tell him to let Dutch go and to stand up."

Kwong spoke in Cantonese, and the man let go of Dutch and rose slowly, his eyes riveted on Lees' revolver.

"Ask him what they were trying to do," Lees said.

Again, George spoke to the uninjured Tong member, who answered, his head nodding, and his smile beaming back at them.

"He says they saw two white men taking a Chinese somewhere. That's it. They wanted to rescue me," said George.

"Tell them you're already rescued and to get the hell out of here," Lees said, flashing his badge at them from under his cape.

After George spoke to them, the two men in black hobbled off, the uninjured one assisting his partner down the alley.

"You see why we can't have any of those Tongs around the mansion? They're all crazy as hell," Dutch said.

"Again, before we were so rudely interrupted, take George to Nob Hill. I'll meet you there in about an hour, after I report his escape." Lees began to walk down the alley back toward the district station house on Kearny.

***

Inside the mansion, Clara was at the table, drafting the advertisement she was going to include in the daily San Francisco newspapers. Ah Toy was painting beside her, swathing her brush with blue on the canvas depicting a steamship coming into San Francisco Bay. The moon was full outside and was shining into Ah Toy's abode. Each woman, at different moments, looked up to gaze at the moon in reflection.

"Carrie, do you love him?" Ah Toy asked, adding some black to the steamship's deck.

"We don't know each other. Besides, we're both working now. There has been very little time to become really close. He does fascinate me, I must admit. A man of his stature should have been married by now. Do you think it's just because of his dangerous line of work?" Clara stopped, wrote down enough to finish her paragraph, and looked up at the moon.

"You are in just as much danger. I think it may be that very danger that has drawn you both together. Perhaps it will pass when this case is over."

"Listen to what I have written. You'll be teaching it, so you should be aware of how I am selling your skills." Clara smiled. "In 1884, women have few ways to earn a living. Come to our personalized appointment to see if you have the aptitude and the fortitude to benefit from our instruction. Learn from a woman who has become independently wealthy through her own initiative. She can teach you how to manipulate the patriarchal system that rules society. It's the only way women can succeed in today's oppressive business atmosphere." Clara held the paper up and blew on the wet ink. "Well, what do you think?"

Ah Toy set her paintbrush down, minced over to the table and sat down next to Clara. "I like it. However, don't you believe it would be prudent to inform these people that I'm Chinese?"

"Perhaps. After we've trapped the killer. You see, I believe this monster has moved out of the Chinatown hunting grounds. Since we're located in the Hopkins Mansion, the killer might even believe he or she can murder somebody white and wealthy. This would be an important status improvement." Clara took her friend's hands. "Because I am the only one who knows who this murderer is, I will have to be present during all of the interviews."

"All right. I understand that. You mentioned—or somebody mentioned—that the killer may be wearing a disguise. How will you be able to identify this person? Also, don't you think he or she will have to kill us both?" Ah Toy raised her eyebrows and squeezed Clara's hands.

"Of course. That would be mandatory, under the circumstances. But don't worry, Ah Toy, I have a few ways to physically recognize our culprit. This person has a large mole on his right cheek, and a cleft in the chin. I've already informed Captain Lees and his men."

Ah Toy stood up. "We had better leave now. Our men should be returning with Bai Kwong soon. I really enjoyed the excuse you gave to Mrs. Hopkins and the servants as to what will be happening when they bring another Chinese into the mansion."

"I think it stands to reason, don't you? You're an artist, and your subject matter features everything Asian. We have employed a few models for your use. You'll be creating your masterpiece. *Chinese Lawbreaker*. George shall be the young miscreant, and Captain Lees and Detective Vanderheiden will pose as the arresting officers. I believe even Shakespeare would approve of this extra bit of ironic art within our larger play." Clara stood up and walked with her friend to the door.

"This will be art imitating life." Ah Toy smiled.

***

The evening fog was rolling in as Dutch escorted George Kwong onto Sacramento Street leading up from Chinatown to Nob Hill. They then crossed over to California Street and arrived at the Hopkins Mansion. It was a steep incline, and they were both winded when the guard at the mansion finally let them through.

The man servant, Hannigan, met them at the front door. Taking a cue from Ah Toy, he shouted up the stairs, "Miss Ah Toy! Your models are here! Shall I escort them up to the Observatory?"

Ah Toy and Clara were standing on the second floor. Ah Toy looked through the spiral staircase leading down to the main entrance and saw Hannigan standing with George Kwong and Detective Vanderheiden. She cupped her mouth and shouted down, "We'll meet you there." Both of their voices echoed back-and-forth through the dark and eerie mansion like wailing ghosts.

***

Back at the Jenny Lind City Hall station, Captain Lees had informed Sheriff Connolly of the escape of his prisoner. Although he fumed, and immediately wired the mayor, Washington Bartlett, Connolly seemed to have accepted the logic behind Kwong's escape. He even understood the ruse about not wanting to fire at the fleeing prisoner because of the many tourists in the streets, although he had his own perspective. "You should have shot anyway, Lees," Connolly barked. "What's a few dead suffragettes? They make more trouble than they're worth."

After the mayor's office was in communication with Connolly, all hell broke loose. The sheriff began running around the bullpen, shouting orders, and slamming his fist on the desks of the officers.

As he burst open the door to the Chinatown Squad Office, he discovered his protégé, Jesse Brown Cook, on his knees with a young uniformed officer. They were praying. "Get up, Cook! That chink Kwong is on the loose! He broke away from Lees and Vanderheiden on the way to see Doc Reed. Mayor Bartlett wants a dragnet on the whole city. He probably took off for chinkville, so you take your men and comb every building in that infested pig sty. Start with Andrew Kwong's place on Sacramento."

"Don't worry, Sheriff," Cook said, as he strapped his holster around his waist and pulled on his tiger hat. "We'll root out that godless murderer. I know every secret hiding place in Chinatown."

"I'm going to find my partner, Sheriff. If he's recaptured Kwong, or knows where he's headed, I'll be back to inform you." Lees watched Cook as he herded his men near the door. He thought they looked like clowns in P. T. Barnum's Greatest Show on Earth. They were certainly clumsy and ineffective, as they pushed and shoved each other going out into the street. Lees followed them out, chuckling to himself.

***

Inside the Observatory room, Clara and Ah Toy were busy discussing how they were going to carry out their ruse. George Kwong, of course, needed new clothes, although his jail garb was explained by the role he was going to be playing as a model for the *Chinese Lawbreaker* painting. Hannigan had seen much stranger goings on working for the eccentric Mrs. Hopkins, including live peacocks strutting throughout the halls, and a troupe of Chinese acrobats. He was happy to go get the new clothing for George.

"Thank you, Hannigan," Ah Toy said.

When the butler left, Ah Toy turned to Clara. "You have to realize all that you have done, Carrie. You are saving your client's life, but you are also showing other women what can be done if you believe in justice and human rights. So much of the world is dominated by power and influence and not by principles," Ah Toy said, as she set up her easel and color palette under the skylight.

"I understand, Ah Toy, but my mind works the same way Captain Lees thinks. We concentrate on the task at hand and not on the glory to come." Clara turned to Vanderheiden. "Detective Vanderheiden. What happened to you? Your suit is stained with dirt, and you have scratches all over your face."

Dutch looked at Clara as if he were the boy who was caught pilfering the cookie jar. His face reddened, and he tried to sweep the stains off with his hands. "We were in a little scrape in a Chinatown alley. The captain saved my life. We was attacked by a couple of Tong boys who thought we were kidnapping George here. I guess I wasn't looking and got tackled."

"Captain Lees disarmed that hatchet-wielding thug by using his Bowie knife. He dropped down low, like an Indian, just as the intruder rushed him, and he sliced the Tong's Achilles tendons. His assailant went down like a puppet that just had his strings cut. Wham!" George Kwong spoke with the colorful phrases of his journalist's skill.

"Did I hear my name being used in vain?" Captain Isaiah Lees stood in the doorway, scowling.

In spite of herself, Clara rushed over to Lees and gave him a demonstrative hug. "Thank goodness, you're safe!"

Lees gently pushed Clara away. "What did you ladies concoct about our being here? I was thinking about that on the way over."

"Clara thought of an excellent ruse. I shall be painting your portraits in the Observatory. You and Detective Vanderheiden will be arresting young Bai Kwong, who will be dressed in his jailhouse uniform." Ah Toy explained. "She even thought of a title for my masterpiece."

"The One that Got Away?" Lees laughed.

"How dare you insult my creativity!" Clara chuckled. "I entitled it *Chinese Lawbreaker*. It will show the pathos of such a young man being taken in, not having a chance in the world against the powers that be."

"Indeed. You should have seen this powerful one with his face down in the alley mud," Lees said. "As for myself, after all of this is over, I may be the one being arrested in your painting. I'm up to my eyeballs in this illegal subterfuge right now."

"The subterfuge must continue, I'm afraid," Clara said, moving over to the table and picking up her advertisement. "I now have the content that will lure our killer from hiding and into our haunted mansion. The ghost of all these murdered women shall assist me in the capture of such a predator!"

"You will not be alone in this. But it won't be ghosts. You're going to have an armed guard in hiding during every one of your so-called private interviews. We don't even know if this killer will be induced to come into the middle of your spider web. What if he or she attempts the daring deed while you are out and about, or even somewhere else in this house?"

"The captain's right. A smart killer would expect a

trap. We need to plan for all the possibilities," Dutch pointed out.

"What? Do you propose we have a police officer in every room of the house and following me everywhere I go? What if this murderer just wants to kill any woman? Ah Toy, me, or even old Mrs. Hopkins might be in danger. Can you protect all of us at the same time?" Clara was using her attorney mind on this conundrum.

"You seem to forget. I was the captain of all detectives in San Francisco. I also have connections with other districts, in other cities. I can have twenty men—all professionals—who can blend in with any setting or crowd. I shall spare no expense when this trap gets triggered. Kwong's life, and our future careers and lives will depend on how well you are protected. In fact, just as you have chosen to protect the identify of this would-be murderer, I am stating that my private detectives shall be unknown to you as well. They will be there, but you won't know it." Lees placed his hands on his cape and puffed out his broad chest. "Agreed?"

Before Clara could answer, a shout came from downstairs. It was Hannigan.

"Miss Ah Toy! You must come down here. There are hundreds of people assembled by the guard's gate outside."

When everybody, with the exception of George Kwong, assembled out in front of the mansion, the sight they took in was at once frightening and comical. There were indeed hundreds of people out beside the guard house on California Street. The guard, in his plumed regalia, was attempting to ward off belligerent members of what was left of the San Francisco Vigilance Committee. The men were pushing and shoving against the gate, causing it to balloon inward like a fishnet on the wharf, bursting with the day's catch.

The spokesman for the group, a tall, elderly gentleman with a walrus mustache and a Confederate uniform from his Civil War days, was shouting at poor Mrs. Hopkins, who had placed herself in harm's way in front of this person's flailing arms.

"You chink-lover! We know you have that killer inside. Bring him out here, or we'll go in and get him!" the old man shouted at the old woman.

The guard, in his protective stance, stood between the two, his rifle pointed at the Confederate impersonator. Having served in the Union, Mrs. Hopkins' old guard was none too patient with such a scallywag. "Step back, you blackguard, or I'll shoot you between your rebel eyes!"

Stepping back, the old man raised his voice above the crowd's yells. "See? She's got a union-buster guarding the plantation. We need to get that murderer ourselves!"

Clara, who noticed there were also many of her fellow suffragettes in the crowd of demonstrators, sprinted out to the guard shack, with Lees and Dutch following close behind. She could hear poor Mrs. Hopkins speaking to them in her nonsensical manner.

"There are no guided tours to my home without prior arrangements. All of you! Leave at once, or I shall have the mayor call out the National Guard!'

Clara took her position beside the old woman. "Listen to me. Everyone, Miss Ah Toy, the artist, is the only Chinese person living here." She pointed to her friend, who was still standing on the front porch of the mansion. "We will be conducting a course to teach women how to become independent and wealthy in these trying times. Why would we risk our reputation by harboring an escaped felon? I was just going to place my advertisement in the daily news. See? Here it is!" Clara held up the handwritten paper.

Lees moved forward to stand beside Clara. He opened his cape to show his sheathed Bowie, and the Colt .45 in his holster. "And my men and I will be here to guarantee that these courses are respectfully and peacefully attended."

Just as Clara expected, the hundreds of women in the crowd began to scream and applaud the news. They had obviously followed the men up California Street when they heard about the rumor of the escaped criminal. "Clara Foltz! Hail, Portia of the Pacific! We want independence for women now!"

"Follow me, independent women!" Clara yelled, stepping past the frustrated Vigilantes. "I'm going now to place my ad, and I want you with me to protect me on my journey!"

The big crowd opened up, like the Red Sea for a female Moses, and Clara began to strut down California Street toward the office of the *San Francisco Examiner*. The women, in their colorful dresses and twirling parasols, swung in behind her, as if they were modern Israelites following their leader to the promised land.

Behind them, the small crowd of men continued to growl their dissatisfaction at Lees and the guard, but they soon began to disperse, like whipped canines, and began to head back down the street, their invisible tails between their legs, into the waiting fog below.

***

Mayor Washington Bartlett was pacing his office like a caged tiger. The dragnet on his city had commenced, and he was ready to make a speech to the people at the city hall, on the Market Street side. Of course, it was the Van Ness side that concerned him most, but because most of the votes came from the masses, he wanted to assuage them about the danger of their community, while putting the most protection in the Nob Hill and Rincon Hill areas where the rich lived.

The window of his office opened up to a large enclosed platform overlooking Market and the Sand Lots area. There were already thousands gathered to hear the news of what was happening to make the city safe again. Part of them were disappointed that there would be no hanging up on Russian Hill, others were concerned for the safety of their families, and a minority, including former members of the Vigilante Committee, wanted to take matters into their own hands if this mayor proved to be as ineffective as he seemed to be.

Bartlett was ready. He picked up the large megaphone from his desk and held it in his arms as one would hold a baby. It had his last name stenciled on its side in Old English lettering. When he stepped out onto the balcony of his office, the crowd noise was a mixture of cheers and boos. Bartlett brought the voice enhancer up to his full-bearded face and puffy lips, and he began:

"Greetings, fellow citizens of San Francisco. I want you to feel safe this evening because I have ordered a complete search of Chinatown, including the homes of the Six Companies' leaders. I am promising to you, with the authority of my office, we shall have this killer back into custody. He will pay for his conviction of murder in the first degree by hanging by the neck until death up on Russian Hill!"

Cheers were thunderous, but some voices shouted out separate jeering statements, such as "You better get that chink, you crook!" Or, "The Chinese are not the problem, you are!"

"However, I need your assistance to capture this man. If you see or hear anything suspicious, or you see this man," Bartlett held up a large poster with a photo of George Kwong on it, "report it to City Hall or to a local policeman or sheriff's officer. If we work together, we will capture this convicted murderer and keep our city safe, as it should be. Thank you, ladies and gentlemen, and I bid you a good evening!"

Mayor Bartlett turned away from the crowds and walked back into his office. Sheriff Pat Connolly was there to greet him. "Well, what is it? Did you find him?"

"Old Reb Bill and his men tried to scare them with threats. Guess who was staying there with the chink, Ah Toy." Connolly brushed a few bits of cigar tobacco off his Chinatown Squad jacket.

"Clara Foltz?" Bartlett guessed.

"Yes, the chink-lover was there. So were Captain Lees and his Dutch sidekick."

"Oh, really? I want somebody to infiltrate that house and find out what they're up to. I don't care what you do. Tell them there's an epidemic of the plague. Just get inside that mansion and see if they're hiding Kwong!"

"Yes sir!" Connolly saluted and left the room.

"I know he's in there," Bartlett whispered to himself after Connolly left. "If I get him, I can begin to pack my bags for the governor's mansion."

Chapter Nine: The Interviews

One Nob Hill, Hopkins Mansion, San Francisco, March 2, 1884

Both Clara and Captain Lees perfected their individual jobs before the first interviews were to be conducted that afternoon in the mansion. Clara, realizing she may not have written enough in the advertisement to infuriate the real murderer sufficiently, decided to write an article to emphasize the content of the course to be taught to women. She wrote that the course would be an "empowerment for women, in that it will show females how to establish legitimate businesses based on using women's feminine attraction to make money off men, mostly bachelors. It will not be prostitution (no physical contact), but it will include allure, poetry, dancing and other forms of female sensuality and grace."

Clara believed her new article's content, published the day before in the morning papers, would enrage the killer most profoundly because this course will be making "honest women out of former prostitutes in Chinatown and elsewhere." As a result, Ah Toy would become the target for murder rather than some random woman who might show up for an interview.

Clara knew that Isaiah had decided he would import his guardian detective force by giving them staff employment. They would take jobs such as butler, chauffeur, cook, and even maid. The "maid" idea came from Dutch, who believed the killer might let down his guard if he thought it was a woman in his presence. Detective Tom Whitefeather, who looked rather effeminate because he was a beardless young man from the local Muwekma Ohlone Tribe, volunteered for the maid role. Although Tom received some number of good-natured cat-calls and insults, it was soon clear that Tom was so certain of his masculinity that wearing a maid's dress was not threatening to him. The Colt .45 tucked into his girdle would be threatening to any would-be attacker.

There were four women who made reservations to be interviewed that afternoon. Clara was on pins and needles about their possible identities. She had once again gone over the clues she had collected to lead her to the killer. She also knew the two physical traits that she could use to identify this person. Hopefully, this information would be enough to save Ah Toy's life and possibly even her own.

The day before, when she was taking her new article to the newspapers to be published, she also sent a message to her family in San Jose at the telegraph office on Market Street. She did not want to unduly frighten them about what she was about to do, but she did want them to know she was thinking of them at this time of personal crisis. She imagined it was like her husband, Jeremiah Foltz, the Civil War veteran, who told her about how painful it was to go off to battle.

"Carrie, I am not the same man I was because of what I saw. I cannot trust society ever again."

If Jeremiah had become so mentally affected by his war experience, then what was she going to be like after confronting this demonic woman-killer? Would she have to pull the trigger? If she did, and this murderer were dead, then would the evidence she had be enough to convince the mayor and the police? Writing down the message to her family was a brief respite from such thoughts:

How are my beloved ones? Are they growing like beanstalks? I so long to have you all in my arms once more! I am working hard to make it so. As soon as I have saved enough, you shall be escorted to me by an entire police force. I am doing important things, as you may have read, Father, and now I will be tested. Do not fear. I will make the most of my trials, I will soon call you to my side for the rest of our lives together! Yours lovingly, daughter and mother.

Now that Clara was mentally prepared for this ordeal, she went about setting up Ah Toy's room for the first interview. Ah Toy would be seated at the table facing the door. The person being interviewed would enter through the facing door and would sit in the padded green antique chair, which had no armrests. This was to give Clara and the guard easy access to shoot the killer if he or she should pull a gun while seated. Detective Vanderheiden discovered that the late Mr. Hopkins used an ingenious two-way mirror in his study to observe prospective business partners before meeting with them. When the lamp light was shined on the rear side of the mirror, where Clara was, it became transparent, and she could secretly view the suspect. She knew she must be able to identify one or both of the physical traits of the suspect before preparing for the arrest.

The staff and integrated detective force were instructed by Captain Lees to never discuss George Kwong or even the fact that Ah Toy was going to paint a portrait of him in the Observatory steeple. The escapee's presence in the Hopkins mansion must remain a guarded secret until the real killer was captured or terminated. And, most importantly, no guard was to confront or attack a person visiting the house unless Clara gave the word. They all knew about the physical traits of the suspected killer. Lees and Vanderheiden would appear at the mansion during the scheduled interviews in the afternoon.

The four women to be interviewed were Miss Marjorie Potter, Mrs. Elizabeth Baxter-Shaw, Miss Changying Chen, and Mrs. Miriam Levine. Two were single women and former prostitutes who wanted to begin new lives. The others had been married, but Baxter-Shaw was a widow, and Levine was divorced.

Miss Potter arrived promptly at one in the afternoon, and Hannigan brought her upstairs to Ah Toy's office and living quarters. Clara was in the adjoining bedroom, peering through her mirror at the entering applicant. The distance between the suspect and Clara's eye was ten feet. She could see the woman's face, and Clara knew at once this person was not the killer. Even disguised, Clara knew she wasn't the one. Miss Potter was too diminutive. She was an attractive young lady of about twenty-five, with auburn hair rolled into a bun, an hourglass figure, and a professional dress that included a fashionably dark-blue, narrow skirt with a medium bustle. Clara listened to the interesting dialogue between her friend and the young applicant.

"Miss Potter, I want you to forget about your past and especially how you came to your profession. What I need to know is why you want to learn how to work as an independent woman." Ah Toy leaned forward, watching the way the woman conducted herself as she spoke. From her many years supervising young women, Ah Toy had three key questions that she answered by watching and listening: 1. Did she look you straight in the eyes? 2. Was her grammar and elocution proper? 3. Did she have a sense of humor? If a candidate failed in two of the three questions, then she was rejected, even as a prostitute working for Ah Toy in Chinatown.

Miss Potter gazed steadily at Ah Toy as she spoke, her eyebrows arching somewhat at emotional moments, her tone calmly confident.

"I want to learn to become independent because our society respects those who can make life better by contributing to values we hold dear. As you stated in your advertisement, a woman who knows how to benefit from the finer attributes of life like literature, dance and physical magnetism, can profit without losing her chastity. I have known this to be true, even when I dreamed it during what I now call my fallen days. I watched these women of grace and allure as they paraded in the hotels, and I tried to be like them in both appearance and voice. Sadly, I did not know there were women like you who could save me from the burden of masculine lust and fear that was used to keep us submissive and dependent on our keepers. As I rode the cable car from downtown, I kept feeling inside as if I were climbing up to a woman's Mt. Olympus, where I could finally learn the skills we need to survive the rape of Zeus. Zeus overcame most of his female victims by trickery: he raped Leda in the form of a swan, Danaë in the guise of a golden rain, and Alkmene in the persona of her legitimate husband, and he did not even hesitate to take on so coarse a disguise as that of a randy satyr for the purpose of violating Antiope."

Ah Toy laughed. "My goodness! Where did you learn about Greek Mythology?"

Miss Potter bowed her head in embarrassment, but then she looked up again, and smiled, her blue eyes flashing. "I often acquired my best clients at the library. I had the time, so I read about the foundations of our democracy. The Greek Pantheon was dominated by gods who would fulfill their needs through trickery. I asked myself, if they could do it, then why couldn't we women? Until I read that ad in the newspaper yesterday, I thought it was impossible."

As Clara watched her friend interview the young candidate, she had a deeper awareness of why she loved the United States and its Constitutional experiment. In theory, every person, even a woman such as Marjorie Potter, should have the opportunity to rise above her bad luck and birth right to build a new life. Just as Clara had overcome the infamy of desertion and divorce, so, too, could Marjorie overcome the depression and dangers of harlotry. In America, we must help one another, and we must fight the tyrants who would keep us down for their own manipulative purposes. To do this, our Constitution must be flexible and adapt to new conditions and it must protect our downtrodden and powerless. Laws such as the Chinese Exclusion Act were not in keeping with our Constitutional tenets of "equality and justice for all."

Mrs. Elizabeth Baxter-Shaw also arrived on time at two, but it seemed she was attempting to complain to Ah Toy rather than the established protocol. A recent widow, the applicant wore a scarlet and black satin dress, and a tall, turban-like matching hat that perched on top of her graying black swirl of hair like a buoy in the San Francisco Bay. She also held in her arms, cradled like a baby, a tiny black chihuahua. A tall Negro chauffeur was carrying her black parasol, and he also took the dog from her, as the

147

missus sat down in the chair while keeping up a constant stream of diatribe.

" ... and then the cable car conductor began to lecture me about bringing a receptacle for my dog's feces. I pointed to Abraham, my driver, and I told the little man that he was my six feet two inches of receptacle. We drove out to the California Street station in a surrey, only to be insulted by a pipsqueak in a uniform. Our conductors on Rincon Hill are much more decorous to their betters. It must be the steep incline, don't you think? Blood must rush too quickly into their brains. Do you believe in the hidden influence of magnetism?"

Clara briefly surveyed the face of this chatterbox, saw that she was not the killer, and tried to keep from giggling out loud at the woman's audacity. She had known many such women--usually wives of judges or important men in the state legislature--and they often became eccentric after their spouse's passing. However, Mrs. Baxter-Shaw was one of the most humorously flamboyant she had ever met.

"Thank you for coming, Mrs. Baxter-Shaw. I want you to tell me why you want to learn to become an independent woman." Ah Toy covered her mouth with her hand, leaned back, and exhaled, poised in uncomfortable anticipation.

"Now that Reggie's gone, I wanted to find some unique way to occupy my time. I read your strange advertisement, but since I have already established myself as a femme fatale, by going through four husbands, I thought I might be able to help you train younger women in the fine art of seduction. Why, when I entered the mansion, a man had the nerve to wink at me!"

Clara was watching the Negro. When his employer

said "seduction," a faint grin widened the corners of his mouth, and he coughed into his hand. Clara also knew that the winking man was Dutch Vanderheiden.

"I am also an art collector. I know you're an artist, and certainly Mrs. Hopkins knows fine art, so perhaps we can become women who can influence men with our tastes. My second husband, the judge, used to send me all over the world to collect art for him."

Yes, he probably wanted to get rid of you, Clara thought. She watched Ah Toy lean forward, waiting for the opportune moment to interrupt the widow.

" ... I remember, it was a cold day on the hill, and I was gazing out my luxurious bay window at the setting sun. The disappearing sun so reminds one of the sad time when your husband is off on another business ..."

"Thank you, Mrs. Baxter-Shaw. We will get back to you following our assessment." Ah Toy took a deep breath and shouted, "Hannigan!"

Clara was most suspect of the third candidate, as she was late to the interview. She asked Ah Toy to conduct the interview in English, if at all possible, and she agreed. Changying Chen arrived at half-past three. She had, like Ah Toy, bound feet, so her gait was impeded. She was breathless as she minced into the room and sat down in front of her interviewer. The *cheongsam* she wore was blue silk, plain and business-like, and, as Clara surveyed her facial features, she was relieved to see none of the telltale signs of the murderer. The young woman's smiling face was full and healthy, and her clear brown eyes were fixed on those of Ah Toy, waiting, with her small hands folded in her lap, for her interviewer to speak.

Ah Toy first spoke to the young woman in Cantonese. Getting an immediate response in perfectly

149

enunciated English, Ah Toy continued in English.

"I do not want to hear about your past or your negative experiences in the profession from which you wish to escape. Please answer this one question. Why do you want to learn how to become an independent woman?"

Bowing her head of short raven hair, she spoke in a voice that was clearly loud for an Asian woman. "Please, may I be bold, like the crane fishing at low tide on the Yangtze? I am so sorry for being tardy. I was forced to climb California Street because Chinese are not allowed to ride the cable cars. To the kept women in Chinatown, the story of Madame Ah Toy is second only to the Goddess Mazu. Our dreams are filled with your exploits, perhaps somewhat exaggerated over the years, but their import remains the same. If we can remain sane and fix our purpose to your lodestar, we may survive another day. That is what I have done. After six hundred and fifteen of these days of survival, I awoke to read in *The Oriental* that my personal morning star was in San Francisco to share her wisdom. It is my great fortune to be here. So many of my sisters cannot escape the Tong dragon's fire, but perhaps I can be their representative. If I am chosen, I will share my skills to those who also wish to become independent. Madame Ah Toy, I am your obedient servant!"

As Clara watched and listened, there was only one moment when she was struck by what she saw. When the initiate bowed, fixed in the back of her hair was a silver comb in the shape of a seahorse. The attorney knew she must find out where Changying Chen obtained that comb, but she dare not expose herself during this interview. She decided to wait until Ah Toy was finished. When the young woman left the room, it would take her some time to leave the premises because of her bound feet. Clara would therefore be able to instruct her partner about what she needed to know, and Ah Toy could call her back, and Clara could slip back behind the mirror.

After several more minutes of conversation, Ah toy stood up. "I believe you will fit nicely in my class. I will send you the curriculum next week. I'll have Hannigan escort you to the door."

The butler came at once when Ah Toy shouted, and Clara came out of hiding as soon as the door was closed. "Ah Toy, you must call her back and ask where she obtained the silver comb in her hair. Each of the murder victims had this seahorse comb fixed in her hair. She might be the next victim, but I need to know where she got it. I will hide behind the mirror until you find out."

Now it was "Changying" that Ah Toy shouted down the shadowy stairs of the mansion. After a few moments, Ah Toy could hear the young woman's lumbering steps climbing toward her. After she was back inside, the older woman asked the young prostitute where she was able to procure such an interesting hair clasp. Ah Toy explained that she collected them from all over the world.

"My handler in the San Ho Hui gave it to me as a gift when I left him to become independent. He was one of the rare benevolent Tong members, and I was very fortunate to have had him as my protector. He even told me once that I had the special intelligence to become an independent woman like the great Ah Toy. I consider the comb a talisman of good fortune."

When Clara heard Changying's response, she was immediately relieved. There would be no need to take the drastic action she thought might be necessary.

There was one remaining woman to be interviewed

that day. None so far had been the suspect. Clara realized that perhaps her killer might be too fearful to take the bait. Before the last interviewee was to arrive at four p.m., the two women attended to their personal hygiene.

Captain Lees brought Clara and Ah Toy some food. A tray of fruit and bread. He asked them how the interviews had gone.

"Two of the three women have been selected. All is not lost. I thought I might have our next victim, but it turned out to be a false alarm." Clara took a bite of the red apple. "Have you or your men seen anything suspicious around the mansion?" She asked, in-between chews.

"Nothing untoward. Those Vigilante old-timers haven't reappeared. Good riddance. George Kwong is still safe and secure in his ivory tower." Lees jerked a thumb at the mirror. "How has that been functioning for you?"

"I must say, it's an excellent way to spy. I can see persons in the room very clearly, and the sounds are quite acute. I should think you might consider adopting it for your detective needs, Isaiah," Clara said, tossing the apple core into a trash receptacle beside the desk.

"You have one more person to interview today. I must speak to Clara alone before this happens. I want to discuss the strange goings-on at Connolly's office. My spies have been keeping me informed."

"Very well, Isaiah. Ah Toy, would you be so kind as to leave us alone for a short while?" Clara walked to the door and held it open for her friend. She noticed that Ah Toy smiled at her and winked as she minced past her.

"Why have you been on a suicide mission?" Lees was standing before the two-way mirror, staring into it. "I can never reach you, try as I may. You and I might as well each be on either side of this blasted mirror!"

Clara was taken aback by the anger in her new paramour's voice. It was the first time he had confronted her the way she expected most men to behave. Force had never been a way to win her heart, and she wanted to prove to him that her quest for independence extended to him as well.

"I am experimenting, former Captain of Detectives. I have not worked at this sleuthing business as you have for decades. What do I really mean to you, anyway? You must have many young women you meet all over town. Why choose me? I have five children, and I value my solitude because I want to help other women break the bonds of control that you men have enforced for so long!"

She saw by the redness in his neck that she had possibly extended her venom too far. He stepped toward her, gazed fiercely into her eyes, and held onto her shoulders as if he were arresting some common street thug.

"Good lady! I have lost my job over you. I have also risked arrest and banishment from these streets. As for other women, I have not shown love for any woman since I was a lad back in England, and there it was my own mother to whom I displayed such affection. If anyone is being manipulated in this dalliance, it is I!"

By the tears in Isaiah's eyes, Clara suddenly realized why this man, this captain of detectives, always had a scowl on his face. All of his energy, all of his personal grief at sympathizing with the downtrodden, was caused by his inability to become intimate with a female. He, in his valiant effort to become the perfect policeman, had remained a virgin for over forty years!

"Don't you see, Clara? I want to save you. You are so unique. So beautiful and refined. And your independence is what attracted me to you. I don't wish to marry. I just want to be with you to share your heart's desire."

Clara felt Isaiah's hands loosen their grip, and she stepped into his arms, allowing him to encircle her with his strong biceps. After being treated like a common peasant wife for all those years, married to Jerimiah Foltz, a man-child, Clara finally believed she could at last commit to a real man, who had been waiting for her his entire life.

As it had been with Charles Gunn, Clara was once again in charge of the intimate relationship. However, this time, she wanted the intimacy without being in control. She wanted to teach this older man why her body was so defensive to allowing a man to reach those inner places where love yearns for release. She knew, at last, that she could find complete physical assurance with a man, and she began to kiss his neck, pulling him toward the other room where the bed was.

He fumbled with her buttons, and he laughed at the bustle in her dress, and he called her a "humped-back she whale." They both began to laugh. She didn't need to put up a false front of intellectual distance, the way she did with little Mr. Gunn. And, when she was standing naked in front of Isaiah, she helped him undress.

Finally, as he stood before her, he had a stomach paunch of middle-age, but his bare, hairy legs were set wide apart, in the fierce stance of an aging warrior. His eyes were staring at the floor, perhaps grieving one last time for all those years of fighting his inner lust, and the tumescent snake that began to engorge itself before her was unlike any member she had ever seen before. It was a woman's unspoken fantasy.

As he came toward her, she smiled, and all she could do was allow a growl to escape her passionate throat. Perhaps this was why he had never made love to a female. His manhood was something that would strike fear in any young virgin or even a prostitute. At last, she thought, her giving birth to five wonderful children had made her receptive to this final gift of carnal pleasure from a man she could teach, without words, about how a woman could enjoy and reciprocate unmarried bliss.

***

Mrs. Miriam Levine wasted no time when she arrived. She burst through the door to Ah Toy's room, pushed up the bustle on her green satin dress, and plopped down in the chair in front of the desk. Her dark eyes immediately fixed upon Ah Toy's, and Clara believed she also looked up and stared directly at her behind the mirror. The woman was in her forties, and her height and facial features immediately eliminated her from the murder suspect list.

"Thank you for coming, Mrs. Levine. I don't want your history. I only need you to tell me why you want to learn how to become an independent woman." Ah Toy leaned forward in rapt attention.

"No, I am afraid you will both listen to me. I am from the Office of Attorney General of these United States. Our men will soon be entering these premises to recapture the fugitive from justice, Mr. George Bai Kwong. You may now come out from behind that mirror, attorney Foltz. We need you to call off your Captain Lees and his undercover detectives or face arrest for aiding and abetting a fugitive." Mrs. Levine opened her handbag and extracted a badge affixed to a leather holder. She set it down on the desk.

Clara decided she must cooperate, so she opened the door of the adjoining bedroom, and stepped out into Ah Toy's living room. Clara picked up the badge and looked at it. It had the name of Benjamin H. Brewster, the Attorney General under President Chester A. Arthur. She tossed it back onto the desk, thinking about how she would proceed. If her client were taken back into custody, then her trap would have to be put on hold, and the murderer would be free to kill again. Clara couldn't hope that the hangman would be postponed because of such a horror, and George Kwong would die.

"Mrs. Levine, if that is your name, I am certain you must be aware that I am the official counsel for the Six Companies and for the Defendant, George Kwong."

"Of course. My name is Miriam Levine. In point of fact, it is your reputation as a brilliant orator for women's rights that caused Mr. Brewster to forgo the warrants for the arrests of both you and your associates in crime. His wife, you see, is a rather vehement supporter of our cause. As a woman, I was sent to explain the Federal Government's purpose in this arrest of your client."

"He is Chinese. You know that's the real reason," Ah Toy said.

"Miss Ah Toy. I have read about you and your story of success. The fact that Mr. Kwong is Chinese has nothing to do with our being here. We are here to protect him from the likes of Mayor Washington Bartlett, about whom we have done undercover detective work of our own. When we discovered that Mrs. Foltz's story about Bartlett keeping the murders of seven Chinatown prostitutes a secret from authorities was true, we immediately began our plan. We also have revisited the homicide trial in which your client was accused of murdering Miss Mary McCarthy. The fact that you were not allowed to appeal because of your client's status as a non-American citizen should not have restricted his access to a fair trial. As a result, we are taking him into our custody to protect him from the local authorities, about whom we suspect of being biased and politically motivated."

Clara sat down in another chair next to Miriam Levine. She grasped the woman's hands into her own and gazed into her dark brown eyes. "Does this mean we can continue with our interviews? Do you believe my client is innocent of these murders?"

Mrs. Levine smiled. "Of course, counselor. You provided an excellent defense for your client in court. We also believe the killer is still out there, and we shall support your effort to trap him or her, but we cannot allow Mr. Kwong to stay here. It is unsafe."

"I understand. But where will you keep him? If you can't trust the local police, then you must have some other place in mind." Clara was toying with the idea of telling this woman about who she believed the killer was, but she didn't really trust her to do the right thing at this point.

"We can't really divulge that information, counselor. You can understand that also. You kidnapped Kwong once, so we can't completely trust you won't do it again. After all, the killer has yet to be apprehended, and the local authorities are not to be trusted, so there you are. It's quite a quandary, don't you think?" Levine brushed a wisp of black hair from her forehead.

"All right, I'll inform Captain Lees, and we'll go get George Kwong. Will you be allowing the undercover detectives to guard us in the mansion? If this killer does appear, we will need the protection."

"You shall have your protection. We just want to keep your client away from harm until this murderer is found." Agent Levine stood up. She reached over and shook hands with Clara, and she then did the same with Ah Toy.

Ah Toy and Clara took Mrs. Levine up to the Observatory to see George Kwong. When they opened the door to the enclosed, circular room, it was empty. Captain Lees must have kidnapped the young man once more, and Clara was dumbfounded.

"I can't believe it! He was here this morning. Captain Lees told us to meet him here after we finished interviewing for the day." Clara ran around the room, looking in the closets, turning back the bedspread, and peering into the small bathroom.

"I'm certain you realize, counselor, if your friend, Captain Lees, knew we were coming, then he is now a kidnapper and subject to federal prosecution." Mrs. Levine took out a pad of paper and picked a pen out of her handbag. She wrote down something quickly. "I must get a wire off to Washington. The Attorney General must be notified. I'm afraid we will be searching for Captain Lees and your client. When we find them, there will be due process of law."

"Does this mean we cannot continue our hunt for the killer?" Clara held her breath, clasped her hands to her breast, and stared hard into Mrs. Levine's eyes.

"I must get permission from Washington. I will tell you tomorrow. Until then, you must not permit any more strangers to visit Hopkins Mansion." Mrs. Levine walked toward the door. "I am sorry this had to happen. I respect what both of you are doing, and I wish you the best of luck."

CHINAWOMAN'S CHANCE

***

Tin How Temple, Waverly Place, Chinatown, San Francisco, March 2, 1884.

There was one place that the Chinatown Squad had never discovered. This room was inside the Tin How Temple, beneath the giant statue of Mazu. It was behind a secret trap door in the floor, which opened after the statue was moved to the side. This was where Captain Lees and Detective Vanderheiden had taken George Kwong. When Lees heard about the news that Connolly was spreading about the presence of federal officers in the city, he knew that George Kwong had to be moved again.

Minister Guan Shi Yin had given Lees permission to hide Kwong there, as the young man had contributed greatly in keeping the temple in business. George brought many prostitutes there to pray and to ask the goddess for forgiveness, in an effort to get them back on the straight and narrow.

Inside the room were all the survival accommodations needed to live out a Tong war, or a natural disaster, like an earthquake, or oppression by the city's authorities. Food enough for months was stored inside the lockers in the back of the room, and there was a bed, proper ventilation from a metal shaft that led out to the street, and enough kerosene and lamps to keep the place lit for months. The room had been used by a variety of people, who were being hunted by the police, and Lees and Vanderheiden were the only former policemen ever to be allowed access.

Lees didn't even have to speak Cantonese to Guan Shi Yin, as it was Andrew Kwong, the leader of the Six Companies, who had made all the arrangements for his son to use the secret hideout. As soon as the captain heard about the feds, he simply informed Andrew, and the father of the accused immediately told Lees about the secret room. While Clara and Ah Toy were talking to Agent Levine, Lees and Vanderheiden had taken George Kwong out of the Observatory, through the night streets, and into the Tin How Temple.

"You'll be safe here," Lees told George, as the young man sat on the bed, still wearing his blue jail clothing. "The minister will watch out for you, and we'll be by tomorrow night. I want to tell Clara and Ah Toy about where you are, so they won't be concerned, but I can't chance it until I'm certain there are no feds or local police around the mansion." Captain Lees was standing beside the bed, looking down at his young charge.

"Whatever you think is prudent, Captain. I want to thank you for saving my life once again," George said, his dark eyes glistening under the lamplight.

"Do you think the feds will shut down Clara's trap, boss?" Dutch asked. He was at one of the lockers, rummaging through the foodstuffs, which were mostly Chinese goods.

"I don't really know, partner. However, knowing Clara's skills as a negotiator, I would doubt it. Something tells me the feds came here because of the local corruption and not because of Clara's doings. We really won that trial. You do realize that, correct?" Lees moved over into the light to see the face of Vanderheiden better.

"Win? You do realize that I am a hard-headed Dutchman. I go by what happens and not by what we would like to happen. All I know is that this here kid would be swingin' from a rope if we didn't kidnap him." Venderheiden turned from the locker to face his boss.

"Twice," he added, smiling.

"Yes, well, after this second kidnapping, under the noses of the federal authorities, we may be keeping George company on Russian Hill." Lees returned the grin.

"Do you mind not talking about hanging?" George squirmed on the bed and circled his fingers around his neck. "I had almost gotten used to the confinement in the mansion, and now I am back where I began. I feel like a pawn on the hangman's chessboard."

"Good comparison, lad! I'm happy to see you've kept your journalistic repose." Lees chuckled.

"Listen! You all hear that?" Venderheiden pointed up to the trap door above their heads. The muffled sounds of repeated gunshots vibrated the ceiling floorboards, and dust fell on their heads from above.

"What in the hell is happening up there?" Lees sat down on the bed with George Kwong, and all three men stared up at the ceiling, as the continuing cacophony of gunfire and trampling footsteps made the entire temple rumble like a locomotive was passing through.

After about twenty minutes, the noise finally subsided. Lees and Vanderheiden stood up, and brushed off their clothes, which had become quite dusty from all the commotion.

"You think we should go up there now?" Dutch moved toward the portable wooden stairs that served as the method of getting out of the underground room.

"No. Wait. If it's all clear, then the minister will be opening up that trap door." Lees also shuffled over to stand under the exit with his partner.

"Do you think the authorities know we're even in Chinatown?" George Kwong's eyes were large under the lamplight beside his bed.

161

"Could be," said Lees. "If I know your father, he would do just about anything to save your neck, including starting a Tong war with those authorities."

All three men watched, in rapt attention, as the trap door above them slowly began to open. The sound of the creaking wood seemed like the door to their coffin. Both detectives drew their Colts from their holsters and stood still, pointing the pistols up toward the slowly opening aperture. On the bed, George Kwong held his breath and prayed.

***

One Nob Hill, Hopkins Mansion, San Francisco, March 2, 1884

"Do you have the list of four candidates for tomorrow's interviews?" Clara was having dinner with Ah Toy and Mrs. Hopkins. Their plates contained lamb chops, green beans and mashed potatoes. Hannigan stood to the side, ready to refill glasses of wine and cater to the ladies' wishes.

"Yes, but do you really believe we'll be getting a visit from this killer?" Ah Toy was eating with chopsticks, but she had to first cut her food into small chunks. "You know, back in China, we invented these chopsticks because we were mostly starving. Small bits of food could be picked up easily, and we then had kindling to add to our fire for warmth."

"We'll have no visits from Chinese killers. I don't care if they have chopsticks. Those can be dangerous too!" Mrs. Hopkins shook her gray head, reached over, and snatched the two chopsticks out of Ah Toy's hands. She then stuck them both up into her nostrils. "See?" she grinned. "I could get brain damage from these things."

Clara laughed, but then her face became serious. "I do hope we hear from Isaiah. I'm concerned about where he took our friend George. If he took him back to Chinatown, I don't think Mayor Bartlett will leave a stone unturned until he finds his convicted prisoner."

"We can't be concerned with that right now," Ah Toy pointed out. "We must find this murderer, and that means we have to continue the interviews tomorrow afternoon."

"I am happy we are together in all of this, my old friend." Clara smiled at Ah Toy. "I don't believe I could have done it without your help," she added.

"You once saved my life, Carrie. Remember? If you hadn't defended my business against the San Ho Hui, the little slice on my arm could have easily become a crimson smile on my whore's neck." Ah Toy slid her index finger below her chin, across her neckline. "In our tradition, once your life is saved by somebody, you are responsible to that savior, for life."

"Our Lord and Savior! Halleluiah! Praise the Lord!" Mrs. Hopkins raised her hands in glory.

Chapter Ten: The Killer

One Nob Hill, Hopkins Mansion, San Francisco, March 3, 1884

In order to make herself less of a target, Clara stayed inside the Hopkins Mansion. Ah Toy's room was so large that it had two bedrooms, so it was easy for the attorney to sleep there. When she awoke from a restless dream, in which she experienced herself confronting the killer and being flayed in the manner of the previous eight victims, Clara's mouth was dry, and she probed her body with her fingers, from the neck down, as if it might perhaps be skeletal in form.

No, she was still in one piece, so she got up from the bed, dressed in her blue business frock, with a small bustle, and laced up her high black boots. As she arranged her auburn hair into its usual swirl, she heard something being dropped in the other bedroom. She immediately thought about the killer and, for some reason, about the shadowy figure in the Chinatown alley.

Using the shouting habit she had picked-up from Ah Toy, she cupped her hands around her mouth and let loose. "Are you all right in there?"

"It's me, Mrs. Foltz. Hannigan. Miss Ah Toy's not in at present."

Clara picked up her handbag with the pistol inside and walked over to the other bedroom. The door was open,

164

and Hannigan stood there, having retrieved a statue of a Chinese peasant woman that he had knocked over while dusting. "Top of the mornin', missus. Will you be havin' breakfast up here?"

"It depends. Where's Miss Ah Toy?" Clara tucked a stray wisp of hair up into her swirl.

"She's left to do some art shopping. She said I should tell you she would return before the first interview this afternoon." Hannigan dusted the statue before he placed it back on the wall shelf above the bed.

"Really. Do you happen to know where she's doing this shopping?"

"Yes, I do. I brought her the telegram. It was from Mr. Guan Shi Yin at the Joss House in Chinatown. He told her he would like her to see some rare Chinese artifacts he had for sale. It seems the donations have been few these days, and …" Hannigan began.

Clara's mind froze when she heard the name Guan Shi Yin. She heard nothing more. She grabbed Hannigan's arm, and he stopped talking. He stared at Clara's ashen face.

"Are you ill, Mrs. Foltz?"

Many divergent thoughts raced through Clara's mind at once. Ah Toy, her best friend, had, inadvertently, journeyed into the den of the probable murderer. Captain Lees and his partner were gone. The only reason she didn't tell her friends about the murderer was because if she had told them, they would have wanted to confront him. Isaiah might have even taken the law into his own hands and tried to arrest him. At the very least, the fact the minister was Chinese would have been a death sentence. Finally, and most importantly, she never really knew for certain he was the killer. It was true. That's why she wanted the killer to come to her to attempt another murder. However, there was also the other figure she had seen in the shadows on the day Mary McCarthy was murdered. The flashing blade in the darkness. She still remembered that.

Right now, if Clara told the undercover staff about this, they would certainly storm the Tin How Temple, and, no doubt, Ah Toy's throat would be slit before they could break inside. Was Ah Toy even alive right now? Clara's throat constricted and her mouth went dry. There was only one chance, a slim one at that. She had to go to the temple and confront the killer before he murdered Ah Toy.

"I must leave at once, Hannigan. Could you have someone drive me there by rapid means? It's a matter of life and death, I'm afraid." Clara squeezed the butler's arm until his face winced.

"If you don't mind riding a horse, Mum, Detective Tom Whitefeather has the fastest steed. He won a competition the other day between the mansion staff and the detectives on duty. His dappled gray is a swift mare, indeed." Hannigan smiled., "I'm afraid he won't have time to change out of his maid's outfit."

"I don't care about that. I need to get over to the Joss House right now." Clara ran out of the room and into the hall, and Hannigan followed her. "Mr. Whitefeather!" she shouted. "I need you!"

A short person in a long blue and white dress, with an apron and a frilly white cap, came bounding up the stairs from the first floor. As he came running up to Clara, the attorney understood why Dutch Vanderheiden had thought the native would make a realistic woman. His dark lashes were long and flirtatious, and his hairless chin and jawline, and becoming features, were soft and appealing to the eye. When he spoke, however, his deep bass voice

166

assured her this was no woman.

"Mrs. Foltz. I am at your service. What is your need?"

"I need to get to the Joss House, the Tin How Temple, as fast as possible. Mr. Hannigan says your steed is swift afoot."

"She is. I can take you right now. Please follow me." Whitefeather began to run, and Clara tried to keep up, but she was falling behind as he leaped several steps on the stairs on his way down. When he was standing at the front door, he held it for her as she caught up to him. "Come. She is in the mansion's livery next to the guard house."

Clara tucked her small handbag inside her waist sash. She knew she would soon need the Derringer within. When Whitefeather jumped onto the gray, she realized there was no saddle on the back of the horse. However, the young man was very strong, and when he reached over to extend his arms, she noticed his forearms and biceps bulged against the maid's uniform sleeves like those of a strongman she once saw as a child at the county fair. She gripped his hands, and he pulled her up quickly, until her legs were facing sideways behind him. "Mrs. Foltz, encircle your arms around my chest, and hold onto me. Ghost Lady likes to get her lather up when she runs. Until she's into her full gallop, however, you will experience some amount of bouncing up and down."

Detective Whitefeather did not lie. As they took off in a sprint down California Street, at almost a twenty-five-degree angle, it was, to Clara, what she imagined it might be like riding the mythical Greek horse Pegasus. When they galloped past the streetcar, as if it were standing still, she actually believed the gray ghost horse might sprout wings and fly into the air. Thankfully, they stayed on the pavement, and as they raced toward Chinatown, Clara could feel the wind explode in her hair, sending her skirts ballooning outward to embarrassing proportions.

A strange ancillary to this ride was the reaction of all the suffragettes, who were browsing and strolling down the sidewalks of the city. When they saw Clara and Detective Whitefeather galloping by, at breakneck speed in the middle of the boulevard, they hastily assumed the riders were both female. As a result, they began to cheer and wave, lining up along the street to get a better view.

Clara soon realized these hundreds of women believed this to be a creation of female bravado for their benefit. Never to be lacking for showmanship, Clara dared to grab onto her bonnet with her left hand, and wave it in the air at these boisterous women, and when they saw it was their heroine, Attorney Clara Shortridge Foltz, they began screaming louder, "Portia of the Pacific rides again!" and, "Clara Foltz and women's rights!"

When they arrived in front of the Tin How Temple, there was a large group of Tong gang members standing outside. Standing in their midst was Andrew Kwong, father of Clara's client, George. "Mrs. Foltz! There's been a horrible event. My son is trapped inside the temple. And he is with Ah Toy and your two detectives. Guan Shi Yin has taken them all hostage. My men tried to overpower him, but he had weapons down in the hideout beneath Mazu's statue."

Clara slipped down off the Ghost Lady and stood before the leader of the Six Companies. She took his two hands into her own. "How did Captain Lees and Dutch get overpowered?"

Andrew's eyes were wild, and his voice was cracking. "When someone heard Ah Toy's screams, the

Tongs tried to break into his temple, and the minister fought back with guns he had secretly stored inside the temple. Miss Ah Toy was there with him looking at artwork he had for sale. He had, at first, with my permission of course, allowed Lees and Vanderheiden to keep my son inside the secret room. I never … he's the killer, isn't he, Mrs. Foltz?"

Clara frowned. She was already trying to think of how to save her best friends. "Yes, I've known he was the murderer for some time. I didn't want to identify him until I could trap him into revealing his evil intentions. Of course, I never thought it would come to this."

"He's inside the shrine with them right now. He says he's going to kill them all unless his demands are met." Andrew squeezed Clara's hands. "You must save my son. He is our only child."

"What demands? This man is mentally deranged, and we must be quite certain he has not killed them already." Clara looked at all of the men surrounding them. "You have to get everyone out of here. I want you to translate for me. Let me talk to this man. I must get to the cause of his hatred."

Just as she said this, Clara saw that hundreds of suffragettes were approaching Chinatown from the outer city streets. This wouldn't do. "Get your men to cordon off the perimeter of this street. I can't have anyone making a commotion while I try to negotiate. If the police or federal officials arrive, tell them it's an emergency. I need to talk with Guan Shi Yin alone. I believe I can convince him to let your son and my friends go."

Andrew Kwong moved about the square outside the temple like a man possessed. He gave orders in Cantonese to all the Tongs and other men. The men began to get rope

169

from inside one of the buildings on Waverly Place and string it all around in front of the temple. A guard was posted at every ten feet around the cordon of rope, with a revealing hatchet in his grip.

Nobody was allowed inside Waverly Place. Andrew Kwong escorted Clara up the steps, leading to the temple on the third floor of the building. As she followed the old man up the winding stairs, Clara could smell the pungent odor of burning incense, and cooking stir fry, coming from the clan rooms on the second floor. She felt inside her handbag. The Derringer pistol that Captain Lees had given her for protection was still there, and she fondled its cold metal. She hoped she wouldn't need it, but this man's mental state could now be beyond reason.

"It's right up here." Andrew turned to look at her as they came to the final plateau in the darkened staircase. The only lighting came from holes, in the shapes of different Chinese gods, in the walls of each landing going up. Kwong was now whispering. "I hope I can translate your words so the minister understands them correctly."

"I am certain you'll do well. I have collected some information about your religious practices, but when somebody goes insane, the boundaries of reality and mysticism become disfigured. I'm not quite ready to approach such a task. Any mistake could mean the murder of my friends and your son." Clara climbed the last few steps and stood with Kwong at the door leading into the temple. She could see bullet holes in it from the earlier conflict with the Tongs.

"Shall I?" Andrew asked, as he held his trembling hand on the door's dragon-shaped golden lever.

"By all means." Clara thrust her right four fingers in a forward motion, and she held her breath to calm her racing heart.

When Andrew Kwong opened the door to the temple shrine of Mazu, Clara at once saw the glowing light. It was coming up from the open trap door on the floor of the shrine. The giant statue of the Empress goddess was pushed to the side, and in its place, was the figure of the minister, Guan Shi Yin. He was wearing his golden robes, but it was what he was hovering over that riveted Clara's utmost attention.

His hands were gripping the T-shaped handle of a long metal tube that went down into a square box of some kind. The glowing lanterns from the walls of the devotional chamber were casting an eerie glow on his face, which was smiled at her as he was poised to strike, like some kind of possessed demon.

Clara attempted to keep her voice calm, but the sound still came out with a slight trembling vibration. "Hello, Minister. What are you trying to do? Can we be of any assistance?" Clara could hear Andrew Kwong speaking the translated Cantonese behind her. She then listened, as Guan Shi Yin spoke in a rambling, sing-song response.

Mr. Kwong spoke in a low whisper, "He says Mazu is very angry right now. She has given him the gift of millions of years of oceanic wisdom. The dynamite has been cradled in her gift of Diatomaceous earth, so that it will not needlessly explode until he pushes down on the blasting mechanism in his hands right now. Guan Shi Yin says he worked for seven years as the digger of the graves in Oakland. It was then he learned from railroad workers that there was a much easier method of creating the burial sites in the cemetery. Before the invention of the protected dynamite by Alfred Nobel, it seems Mr. Leland Stanford had forced his Chinese workers to use the black powder explosives. Stanford did not care that many of his coolies were blown to bits, as they carried the charges of Chinese-made explosives out to the mountains where caverns needed to be blown apart to create railway tunnels."

Mr. Kwong wiped sweat from his brow and continued, "But then Mazu created the granulated sea earth which now protects these dynamite charges. At first, the minister says, his friend was killing the women by stabbing them with Guan Shi Yin's sacrificial knife—the same one he used in his tributes to Mazu inside the temple. But then, the brilliant idea came to him. He could terminate the entire prostitution business in Chinatown with one blast and reap a greater reward. This is where we are now, Mrs. Foltz. Guan Shi Yin has connected fifty explosive charges—one for each of our houses of prostitution—and he is going to blow them all if his demands are not met."

Clara's heart began to race again, her brow became wet with beads of perspiration, and her palms were also sweating. "W … what demands?" she managed to blurt out. Also, she wondered, who was "the friend" he was talking about?

"He wants all the houses of ill repute shut down in the United States forever." Kwong raised his eyebrows. "I know, his demands are insane. What can we do?"

"Ask him if I can speak with Captain Lees and Ah Toy." Clara was thinking of a way to work around this quandary. She would need the cooperation of her friends.

Andrew spoke briefly to the minister, who then replied. "He says you can, but you must answer his demands now."

Now? Clara didn't know what to say. If she

promised, would this deranged man even believe her? "Tell him I will contact the authorities I know in the government in Washington. If he lets my friends go, then we can see what develops. We will keep him safe until we can get the decision at higher levels."

Kwong translated Clara's words. The killer looked confused for a moment, but then he smiled, nodded, and spoke to Andrew.

"He says you can speak to your friends now," Andrew told her.

Clara moved closer to the trap door's opening. It was still glowing light from within. She could now see the face of the Asian minister more closely. There were the two physical traits she knew. The dark mole on his right cheek, and the cleft in his chin.

"Isaiah? Ah Toy? Can you both hear me?" Clara shouted. She could feel spittle inside her throat, and she coughed. "Did you hear our conversation up here?"

"Yes." It was Captain Lees.

"Clara, I heard everything," called Ah Toy.

"What happened, Isaiah?" Clara asked.

"He had the dynamite ready when Ah Toy came into the shrine. After the Tongs tried to break into the temple, she was forced down into our room. Ah Toy opened the door, so Dutch and I couldn't get a shot off at him. He has her outfitted as well."

Clara was comforted by the strong voice of her friend. However, she was also confused. "Outfitted? Do you mean he dressed her up in some kind of outfit?"

"No. Not clothing. She is wearing dynamite, which is also fused with his explosive device topside."

Ah Toy had spent many years trying to make her employment of prostitutes safer and less confining. Now, on the verge of teaching women about how to employ their natural charms in a business setting, her best friend and her prospective lover and his partner, were about to be blown apart by this monstrous religious fanatic.

"That's not good, now is it?" Clara became suddenly very calm within. Her voice no longer trembled, her demeanor was slow and perceptive. She believed she was now channeling the millions of years of female survival inside her being. "I'm going to talk with him now. Stay right there, won't you?"

"Don't worry, Carrie," Ah Toy said. "We're not going anywhere."

"Andrew, please translate the following to our minister of the Goddess Mazu." Clara's voice was clear and confident.

"I will do my best, Mrs. Foltz," Kwong said, and he also moved closer to the trap door and the killer.

"Minister Guan Shi Yin, I know your name means hearer of all sufferings. I am going to explain how you will now suffer if you don't release my friends." Clara waited until Andrew Kwong translated. She watched the murderer's face. It became taut, and his jaws clenched. That was a good sign. "I believed you were the murderer of those women shortly after the trial of my client, George Kwong, ended. As a result, I wrote a long dissertation explaining what you had done, complete with evidence that I have gathered, and this written article is about to be sent to all the major newspapers in the world."

Andrew translated, and the murdering minister was now staring at her, his mouth agape in disbelief.

"Oh, yes. If you kill them right now, I have ordered this article to be transmitted by teletype. However, as I do realize you have the upper hands, so to speak, I am willing to make a last negotiation. I know you are a very religious man. I also know I would be the greatest sacrifice for your Goddess Mazu. Why? Because I am the one who has collected all the evidence proving your guilt in these heinous murders. Therefore, if you agree to let me replace my friend, Ah Toy, down in your pit of perdition, I will allow her to destroy my newspaper article. You see, she is the only other person who knows right now where it is. Once she destroys it, she will notify you, and you can release all of us. Is that clear?"

Andrew Kwong took several minutes translating what Clara had said. When the minister spoke, his tone sounded calmer and more deliberate. He punctuated his speech with frequent nods of his head, as he pointed at them with a free hand.

When he was finished, Mr. Kwong turned to speak to Clara, but his face was ashen, and he began wringing his hands.

"He says he never committed any of those murders. It was somebody else who did them. He met this man when he worked in the burial business in Oakland. He says he must have been British, and he knew how to speak Cantonese. A very learned man. He told Guan Shi Yin he would pay him handsomely if he would allow him to stay in the temple's secret hiding place while he practiced his trade in the streets."

"Trade? How can he allow a murderer to practice by taking the lives of young and innocent young women?" Clara's voice was hoarse with emotion.

Again, Andrew Kwong talked to the minister. The translation was finished in several minutes. "He says the man became very efficient, and he allowed Guan Shi Yin to accompany him to each of the killings. The minister helped him get rid of the intestines and other carnage, and he also planted the seahorses as a distraction. Then, the killer told Guan Shi Yin he would pay him ten thousand dollars to blow-up all the brothels in Chinatown. They both believed these women were a blight and a competition with Mazu and the work of Heaven. No woman should be allowed to live in sin and decadence and pollute the holy marriage union with their filth."

"What can I do to convince him to allow Ah Toy to exchange places with me?" Clara pleaded.

The two men discussed this, and finally Andrew Kwong had the minister's answer. "He says the brothels must be blown-up, and he doesn't care about dying. He believes Mazu will reward him by allowing him to enter her virginal and heavenly repose. He will allow Ah Toy to go free so as to report exactly what Guan Shi Yin was able to do today to purify Chinatown of these sinful women. You must, however, place the dynamite belt from Ah Toy around your own waist."

Of course, Clara knew, this insane minister wouldn't be stupid enough to attempt to place the dynamite around Clara himself. "Tell him we agree. Get Ah Toy up here so you can take the dynamite off her and place it around me."

Kwong translated Clara's instructions to Guan Shi Yin. The minister yelled instructions in Cantonese down into the trap door to Ah Toy. After several moments, Clara could hear her friend climbing the rickety wooden stairs up to the floor of the shrine. Clara whispered, under her breath, "Be careful, my sister. Don't trip and fall, for God's sake."

The few minutes it took Ah Toy to climb those steps seemed like an eternity. When she finally appeared at the top step, facing them, her mincing little steps made the tension even more excruciating. She took tiny steps toward them, her silk slippers scraping along the floor of the shrine like sandpaper. Seeing her friend safe and alive was exhilarating.

Ah Toy's face was calm, under the circumstances, and Clara realized her friend had also girded herself against any danger that might assail her. Clara remembered her friend's stories about how female infants in China were often drowned because they were seen to be of no worth to the farmers there. Only the wealthy Chinese daughters had access to dowries. Ah Toy had escaped such punishment by learning to work in the fields at age five.

Clara realized all of these young Chinese women were now expendable, not to mention her own life and those lives of her male companions. As Ah Toy crept forward, in the final few steps, with her mincing gait, the attorney understood just how brave her best friend really was.

At last, Ah Toy was standing next to the minister and his insane explosive device. The shrine of the Goddess Mazu was nearby, in all her golden finery, looking down at this small Chinese peasant woman who had progressed so far in her new home country. Clara believed if Mazu could, she would have patted Ah Toy on the head.

Clara listened, as the minister instructed Andrew in Cantonese on how to take off the suicide belt from around Ah Toy's waist. Finally, her client moved over to stand next to the Chinese woman. His two hands reached out, ever so gently, and unfastened the leather strip that was tied in the small of Ah Toy's narrow back. The three sticks of red dynamite were in a series, and as Andrew brought the strap of leather around with his right hand, these three explosives, which could obliterate the entire Tin How Temple, were dangling in mid-air for several seconds. Clara believed she could hear the three of them as they inhaled slowly and held their collective breaths.

As Andrew was transferring the explosive belt to his right hand, the better to manipulate it so he could bring it around Clara's waist, he dropped it! Clara instantly brought her hands up to her ears, waiting for the crushing blast. Nothing. The minister chuckled and spoke.

Ah Toy translated this time. "He says, Mazu's protective Diatomaceous earth has saved us again. However, it failed to save his son when he was handling black powder for the railroad."

Clara was momentarily struck with empathy. This poor man had harbored a grudge against the powers who took his son's life. This event was the wellspring from whence his insane delusions had come forth. Still, she knew, he was not an innocent. She knew more about his motives than she let on. They were not all delusional.

As Andrew gingerly picked up the dynamite belt, and brought it up to Clara's waist, she inhaled again, as if making her waist thinner could prevent any kind of disturbance.

"Carrie, don't do that. It will be more dangerous when you exhale," Ah Toy explained to her.

Clara let out the air. Andrew, once again, brought the belt around her back and held the two strips of leather between the index fingers and thumbs of both hands. Finally, it was around her, and when Andrew tied it off, Clara began to plan her next move.

Cantonese came pouring from the minister standing at his detonator.

"He wants you to move slowly toward the trap door.

Don't make any sudden moves, or he'll plunge down on his handle immediately. Once you get on the top rung of the wooden steps, tell Captain Lees to assist you. He won't plunge down on the detonator until you're below. It will be your final grave to die together."

Ah Toy was now her personal translator, as Andrew Kwong was still perspiring and breathing heavily from his earlier dangerous exercise.

"Tell him I'll do the best I can. I don't go strolling about the town wearing dynamite every day, you know." Clara smiled, as Ah Toy translated. She was proud of herself that she could keep some humor, in spite of the predicament.

Clara believed it was rather ironic. As she moved toward the trap door in the floor of the Mazu shrine, she was taking the same mincing steps that Ah Toy had to take because of her bound feet. Women in North America were not physically bound, but they were, indeed, legally bound. No voting rights, no rights to own property, the list was quite binding and probably as cruel as having one's feet crumpled up like a cow's horn. As she walked, she slowly moved her right hand to her sash in front of her body. Inside the sash, she felt for the small blue handbag, and she opened it.

She had finally arrived at her destination. The dizziness she felt was momentary, as she looked down into the pit of the hideout room below. In its depths, she could clearly see the face of her new beau. He was looking up at her, an inquisitive expression, perhaps one of respect and care. She had always thought his veneration was what she needed most at this time in her life.

Her five children and her parents in San Jose had always admired her intelligence and her fortitude to overcome obstacles that most women withstood because they believed they were powerless. Clara Shortridge Foltz, however, had never, for one moment, believed she was completely powerless.

"Hello! Mrs. Foltz? Can you hear me?" A voice from outside the temple was shouting at them. It sounded like Mayor Bartlett's voice.

"Yes, we're inside—I'm here as well. Please, don't come in!" Clara yelled, trying not to cause a deadly vibration on her explosive belt.

"But your family is here, Mrs. Foltz. They've come all the way from San Jose to be with you. What's happening in there that you cannot come out?" The mayor's voice was its usual demanding tone.

Clara didn't know what to say. If she yelled again, the explosives might go off. If she told Bartlett about the dynamite, her plan would be ruined, as the mayor would certainly order the police to storm inside. Then, all hell would come to them as Guan Shi Yin plunged down on his weapon for the last time.

"This is Lees, Mayor. Get everybody five blocks away from this temple—right now, dammit! I mean it. If you don't, then their lives will be on your head!"

The sound of running feet outside could be heard, and, as the minutes passed slowly, Clara realized it was once more time for her to act.

Clara exhaled with relief that her family was safe, even though her own life and those of her friends were still at stake. She winked down at Captain Lees, who was standing at the bottom step of the hideout. She saw he was smoking one of Dutch's cigars, and the tip of the rolled tobacco blazed cherry-red in the darkness. It was the first time she had seen him smoke. "Can you assist me,

Captain? I can't seem to get the hang of these steps."

Clara heard the voice of the killer asking Ah Toy to translate. As her friend did so, Clara knew her final moments were upon her. Even so, she wanted to ask the minister one more question. "Ah Toy! Ask him if he knows the name of the man he helped murder those women."

As she listened to her friend talking with Guan Shi Yin, the hearer of all suffering, Clara curved her index finger gently around the trigger of the Derringer, still in her right hand, and she turned around, took a deep breath, and she pointed the pistol at the man who had caused so much suffering in the world.

Had he helped a crazed killer torture and maim eight innocent women, in the prime of their lives, before they even had the chance to mend their ways or had become enlightened as to the ways of this cruel world? Even if he were telling the truth about not being the actual killer, he had definitely chosen to extinguish life instead of protect it, and for that, Clara thought, in the seconds it took for her to aim at his head, he was guilty.

Her talking target was still looking over at the lovely Ah Toy, who was telling him what this white woman was saying. Between that moment, and the moment it took for Ah Toy to speak to the hearer of all suffering, Clara Foltz, attorney-at-law, pulled the trigger, twice—once for her family, and once for all women. The sound that erupted shook her, as if the explosives fastened around her not-too-thin waist had detonated after all.

When his body fell away from the deadly plunger, harmlessly to the floor of the shrine, Clara finally let her breath out in a deep, shuddering wave. Her family was safe, and in her immediate joy, she almost didn't hear Ah Toy's response to her earlier question.

MUSGRAVE

"He said his name was Jack. Jack from London."

Chapter Eleven: Family Reunion

One Nob Hill, Hopkins Mansion, San Francisco, March 6, 1884

One after the other, in the order of their age, all five of Clara's children greeted her in his or her own way. Everyone in her family was there, including her parents, Telitha and Elias Shortridge. They were learning about the recent case and about the new home they would soon be moving into, thanks to the kind benevolence of Mrs. Mark Hopkins. "My big, gloomy mansion," she said, "would otherwise be inhabited by ghosts."

Eighteen-year-old Trella Evelyn came first, and she greeted her mother by giving her a gentle hug and a brief peck on the cheek She wore a new red dress, with decorative designs on the pockets and a big bonnet. No bustle yet, as grandma forbade it. "It's so grand here, Mother. Will I have my own room?"

"Of course, my love. You're a young woman now, and you deserve your privacy," Clara told her, surprised by how tall she had grown in just a year.

Sixteen-year-old Samuel Cortland came next. He wore a frock coat and short pants, and he chose to shake his mother's hand and smile a crooked grin. "Mother, did you plug that rat in the forehead or the temple?"

Clara frowned. "Sammy, never refer to a human

being as an animal of any kind. I had to shoot this man because he could have blown-up most of Chinatown and us with it. It was a matter of life and death, and I really felt a bit sorry for him afterward. Insanity, I now believe, should be determined by a court of law. I was playing judge and executioner."

"Don't you be so hard on yourself, daughter," Elias told her from his seated position on the huge antique living room divan. "You saved a lot of lives that day." Her father's long legs were crossed, and he was smoking a big cigar that Hannigan had given him. Elias wore his best attorney's dark blue suit, with a pink carnation in the lapel of his frock coat. His face was ruddy, his head balding, and his thick mustache was waxy and broad when he smiled.

Mrs. Hopkins, seated to his right, was staring at Elias, reverently, as if he were her deceased husband, Mark. Telitha, Clara's mother, was sitting next to the elderly woman, and she was quite amused by her. She wore a green satin gown that she had worn once to the opera with her husband.

Out on the Persian rug, it was fourteen-year-old Bertha May's turn to greet Clara. She wore a yellow woolen dress with fur at her collars, and her face was streaming tears as she hugged Clara tightly. "Oh, Mama! It's been so horrible without you. Samuel tortures me every day, and I can't find any new friends. My face looks like the craters of the moon."

"My Bertha. This too shall pass. Go sit beside Ah Toy. She will keep you company." Clara pointed to her friend, who was seated on a smaller couch near the fireplace, which was blazing with flames erupting from large winter logs.

Thirteen-year-old David Milton chose to race at his

mother from a standing start. At the very last moment, however, he skidded to a stop, and grinned up at her. "What did you get me?" he asked, holding out his arms. His Lord Fauntleroy short pants and jacket, with matching sailor hat gave him a dynamic aplomb.

"I got you a ride on a gray horse called Ghost Lady!" Clara said.

"Yippee!" David screeched, and he ran off to sit beside Bertha and whisper something in her ear.

Finally, little eight-year-old Virginia Knox skipped over to see her mother. Her blue dress with seven petticoats was quite lovely, and her little round hat had a small blue peacock feather. Virginia stood in front of her mother and stared up at her for several moments, as if she couldn't quite believe it was she. "Are you afraid of wolves?" she finally asked, her hazel eyes big and round.

"I would suppose so! They can hunt in packs," Clara said.

"Will you shoot them for me?" Virginia asked.

"Naturally! And if I don't get them, then my friend Captain Lees will," she added, as she observed that Isaiah had just walked into the room along with his partner, Detective Eduard Vanderheiden. They were both wearing their usual suits, and Lees' trademark gray cape was covering his frock coat.

"I think your mother here is a much better shot, however," Captain Lees pointed out. "By the way, Mrs. Foltz, I was meaning to ask. How did you determine that the Minister of the Tin How Temple was the killer of those eight women?"

"I never thought you would ask, Pinkerton," Clara walked over and gave Isaiah a close hug and a kiss on the lips. She wanted to show her family just how fond she was of this new man in her life. "When you were showing me how to question suspects, I was taking notes, like a good sleuth. I happened to see that in the photos of all the victims, each woman had the same decoration in her hair."

"Decoration?" Lees pulled a red comb from the back of Clara's tresses and held it out for all to see. "You mean, like this?"

"Do I need to decorate this room again?" Mrs. Hopkins pointed to the lamp beside the divan. "I just purchased that lamp from Tiffany!"

Everyone laughed.

Clara continued, "Yes, except these were the same decorations left in all of the victims' coiffures. As a matter of fact, I also spotted those same decorations inside Goddess Mazu's shrine. They were in the trays, which were given as gifts to worshippers who lit prayer lanterns to the goddess. After I had that information, I deduced that Minister Guan Shi Yin must have placed them there after the victims were flayed. It was a sort of gruesome calling card, if you will."

"The silver seahorse combs!" Dutch Vanderheiden remembered. "Sure, boss, why didn't we see those?"

"After Cook arrested our boy George Kwong, I suppose we got distracted. Thank goodness Clara was alert to that which we had passed over." Captain Lees took the red comb from Clara and placed it gently back into her auburn swirl.

"And how did you determine that the minister was working alone? We thought all along that the mayor might be in cahoots with the bee lady at the Home for Wayward Women. Also, what about this fellow named Jack? Do you believe Guan Shi Yin's story about him killing those girls? Or, was it possibly a dark and imaginary doppelganger scapegoat for his sick psyche?" Lees was bringing out all of the questions he had.

"Quite simple, dear Pinkerton. Although Mayor Bartlett had a lot to gain from using the arrest of George Kwong to win the governorship, he had too much at risk and no motive to be part of the murder plot. He dined at the Chinese restaurant, and he worshipped at the altar of Leland Stanford, who was ambiguous about the value of Chinese labor, at the very least. When I learned that the hearer of all suffering once worked in Oakland as a burial specialist, I decided he had the skills necessary to be able to do the expert flaying of our victims. All of the Chinese deceased also had to be flayed before they were shipped back to China for family burials. As for his meeting up with this Jack, I think he was probably thinking about you, Isaiah and your wonderful British accent. You must have impressed him a lot."

Clara saw Andrew and his son, George, come into the room, and she waved at them. "I also knew George Kwong could have never killed any of those women because he was truly in love with Mary McCarthy."

"Now how could you be certain of something as ephemeral as love?" Clara's mother, Telitha, asked.

"He quit his newspaper job after she broke it off with him while she was in the Home for Wayward Women. He did the summer work in Oakland for that lying coroner," Clara explained. "Of course, he did take all the photos of the victims. I think he was emotionally numb by then, and his journalistic work made him immune to their deaths. When his Mary was murdered, I believe he was truly traumatized beyond emotion. Therefore, he became a prime suspect in Sheriff Connolly's eyes."

"Well done!" Lees clapped. "I knew you were a

good student, even though you never graduated from Hastings."

"We women have to make a living these days. Especially if we have to watch out for you men," Ah Toy said, grinning. "Ancient Chinese custom. Get feet twisted to walk daintily for your man. Then he can track you down more easily!"

"I don't want to track anybody down for quite some time," Clara said, opening her arms wide. "Come to me, my glorious family! I want to hold you all in my arms at once, to infuse my soul with your strength. You have done so much to give me inspiration, even though you were far away from me."

All of the Shortridge clan got up and moved to the center of the room to become enveloped in the arms of their mother and daughter. Andrew Kwong, in response, hugged his son, George, and Mrs. Hopkins took Ah Toy into her arms.

Captain Lees and Detective Vanderheiden each wrapped an arm around the other's shoulder and grinned broadly.

David Milton was the first to break away from the group. He ran to the door and stood there, his eyes glowing, and his body shaking with excitement. "I want to ride the Ghost Lady!" he said, bringing his two hands together in front of his chest, and moving them in a rolling motion, as if he were taking off into the sky.

***

Ah Toy's best friend, Carrie Foltz, was able to love again, and her fight against the fear she had of commitment had disappeared with the further enjoyment of Captain Lees' romantic companionship. She told Ah Toy as much, on many occasions, although she knew her

188

friend would probably never be able to commit to the final obligation of marriage. Clara was too much like Ah Toy. She loved her independence more, and they both understood the fight for female equal rights would take a great deal of time and effort to accomplish.

Ah Toy also watched Isaiah Lees, the crusading law man, win against all odds and return to his job on the police force. It reminded her of her days fighting the Six Companies' bureaucracy, and the Tongs had behaved with Ah Toy much like the Chinatown Squad Lees had to go up against to do his job in the city.

Of course, Captain Lees' dear friend and partner, Dutch Vanderheiden, was also reinstated. Ah Toy had always seen them both as an American version of Robin Hood and Friar Tuck, fighting corrupt law and order and giving back to the downtrodden of all races.

Both Sheriff Connolly and his henchman, Jesse Cook, however, were terminated, as all know that excrement flows downhill. Even though the mayor ordered the kangaroo court trial of George Kwong, Connolly and Cook were blamed.

As for the Mayor of San Francisco, Washington Bartlett, the Great White Whale, he, of course, ordered the termination of Connolly and Cook, so he was therefore able to salvage his reputation. Mayor Bartlett, in an irony not lost on the Chinese community, thus went on to win the governorship of the State of California the next year, but he died from Bright's Disease six months into his new administration to fulfill the prophesy of yin and yang.

During Washington's inaugural speech, which Ah Toy read out loud over morning tea and eclairs with Carrie, the former mayor and new Governor of California spoke about the Chinese in this manner:

"While everyone within the jurisdiction of the State is entitled to and should receive the protection of the laws, still the policy of admitting in such large numbers a race who are distasteful to our people, detrimental to our prosperity, and calculated to breed trouble, cannot be upheld, and it is to be hoped that the National Government may heed the remonstrances that have been made and afford the necessary relief."

On the other hand, Ah Toy observed with satisfaction that Six Companies' leader, Andrew Kwong and his son, George, went on to fight the racism and take their case to court, eventually winning their citizenship and the accolades of their fellows, who would soon follow in their legal footsteps. Immigration became a hot issue, and Clara Foltz and Ah Toy followed it closely.

Finally, the man named "Jack," from London, who had been mentioned in that dark temple shrine by a crazed Chinese minister, also headed back to his own country to ply his perfected trade on the Victorian streets of Whitechapel in London's East End. Ah Toy discovered his writings inside the shrine hideaway under Mazu's statue, following the near-disaster, and she passed these important writings on to the authorities. In the killer's journal, he described, in gruesome details, how he had committed the murders and that he envisioned this "practice" would make him "a proficient and jolly good craftsman after his return to England."

Ah Toy enjoyed seeing Captain Lees' and Carrie's reaction when she handed them the written journal of this madman. This last twist in the intricate Chinese puzzle was the only flaw in an otherwise brilliant first trial and investigative premier conducted by a new and imposing young female lawyer, best friend, mother, and detective.

In honor of her own criminology effort, Ah Toy continued to teach women how to benefit from an independent spirit, and Carrie was often asked to guest lecture.

Ah Toy was still living with Mrs. Mary Hopkins and her best friend in the gray whale of a mansion on Nob Hill, and she enjoyed painting almost as much as she did buying and collecting other artists' work and, of course, playing with Carrie's young ones. Perhaps life did, indeed, imitate art. At least, the Chinese believed it did.

Ah Toy watched the fantastic display in this conflicting world and out in nature, as she gazed out one of the bay windows of the mansion, or strolled in her mincing step down the roiling streets of San Francisco. This beautiful Chinawoman loved to show it all, as dramatically as she could, in her art.

Instructional Study Questions

1. Ah Toy, Clara's best friend, had her feet bound back in China. What modern sexist rituals are there in today's world cultures? Do they serve any useful purpose? Discuss.

2. Which scenes best show and demonstrate the psychological manipulation of people? Give specific examples and discuss. How can this be prevented in the workplace or in school?

3. Clara Shortridge Foltz had to tell society that she was a widow. Why did society not approve of women who had been abandoned or who were divorced? Does this exist today? How can society overcome such prejudices?

4. What modern examples of sexist behaviors from work or school can you compare with scenes in this novel? Discuss how they can affect human behaviors.

5. This mystery discusses the way women are judged by men. Give examples of these practices, and discuss how they can be overcome by personal or social laws.

1

As a special bonus, here are the first two chapters of James Musgrave's second mystery in the new Portia of the Pacific series. It's called *The Spiritualist Murders*, and it takes place in 1886 San Francisco, California. We hope you enjoy it and continue to read the new mysteries coming out in this innovative new series of provocative tales. Please join our author's mailing list at emrepublishing.com.

Bonus: *The Spiritualist Murders*

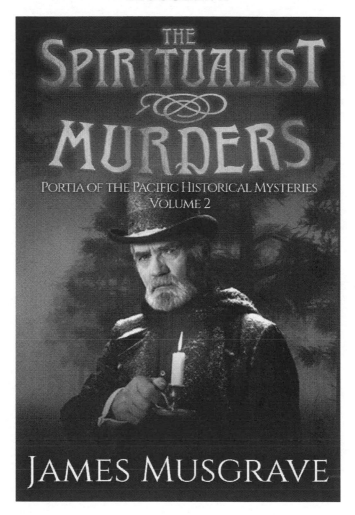

Chapter 1: The Voice

*The Supreme Grand Lodge of the Rosicrucians, 212 Clay Street,
San Francisco, May 2, 1886*

"We grow daily beyond our yesterdays and are ever reaching forth for the morrow. The world has had a long night, as it has had bright days; and now another morn is breaking, and we stand in the Door of the Dawn."—Dr. Paschal Beverly Randolph, *Magia Sexualis*

The young woman sat on the bench in the front row. The Spiritualist gathering place was inside an old Victorian house owned by one of the members, a Mrs. Virginia Partridge. The girl was crying in the fading San Francisco window light that was illuminating her. Her body was folded over, her head in her hands, as she sobbed, her pale-blue bonnet hanging around her white neck by its ribbon.

Clara Shortridge Foltz, Esq., who had been part of the earlier meeting of spiritualists and suffragists, wanted to see if there was something she could do to aid the young woman in her discomfort. With her reddish-brown hair, the girl reminded Clara of her oldest daughter, Trella Evelyn, who was now twenty. Her swirled bun and curly hair was bobbing up and down as Clara walked over to her and placed a hand on her shoulder. The young woman wore a modest blue dress with bustle, and a satin sash encircled her thin waist.

"My dear, what's wrong?" Clara whispered, not wanting to startle her.

The girl was far from startled. She slowly raised her head, and stared into space, her rouged cheeks slick with tears. Her face was pretty, yet Clara noticed she wore dark eyeshadow, and her eyebrows were red smudges above her glistening gray eyes. Clara had seen this type of shaved eyebrows in photographs of Japanese women, who wanted to affect a kind of mystical quality to their demeanor. The girl finally turned toward Clara, folded her porcelain-like hands into her lap, and cleared her throat.

"I don't understand how it happened. I heard the other witnesses, but I still don't believe what they said." Clara noticed the young woman's pupils were constricted, and her words were slurred. The confusing words were perhaps due to a drug-induced condition.

"Witnesses? I don't understand. I am an attorney. Perhaps I can help you." Clara reached down to take the girl's hand, but she pulled back and squealed.

"There were attorneys in that courtroom. All they did was argue about the different witnesses and what they saw. *He* never got called to the stand! He's still out there!" The girl stood up and began humming and shaking her head back-and-forth, as if she were being seduced by a strange, inner demon.

"I can understand why you would want to come to our meeting. We support women's rights under the guise of a spiritual communication. What happened to you? Are you drugged? Were you raped? What's your name?"

The young woman's humming began to transform

into a chanting of words. Clara thought this might be a method of protecting her body. When she spoke, she clutched her arms across her breasts and looked up into the air at some invisible entity, perhaps a protecting angel or a god of some kind.

"Perhaps you can come with me. I don't live too far from here, and I have a friend who knows about the problems of young women such as yourself." Clara took a few steps toward the door, hoping the girl would follow. When she failed to do so, the attorney went back and gently took her arm at the elbow. She guided the young woman toward the door. The girl walked as if she were in another world, looking all about, squinting at the descending sun outside, and continuing to mumble her prayer, if that's what it was.

They took the cable car up California Street to the mansion. The girl seemed in a trance, staring out at the passing pedestrians, horses and merchant carts as if they were phantasms in her personal dream world. Clara realized this when she observed the young woman reach out and attempt to grab one of the passing horses, even though it was at least ten yards from her window inside the trolley.

After getting clearance from the guard at the gate, Hannigan, the butler, answered the tall gray door of the Hopkins Victorian mansion at One Nob Hill. Clara could hear her younger teenaged children roughhousing on the stairs. The Irish butler raised his auburn eyebrows and smiled. "Been that way since you left, Mum. Banshees, they are, to be sure!"

"Could you please tell Ah Toy I want to see her? We'll be in the living room."

"It's nice to get instructions all civilized like. Miss

Ah Toy and her shouts. It's my opinion, Mum, she gets the wee ones all riled up." Hannigan looked over the girl briefly before he turned to leave, the tails of his black coat bobbing against his backside as he climbed the stairway to the second floor.

Clara had been living at the Hopkins residence since she solved the mystery of the eight murdered prostitutes. Her best friend, Ah Toy, the former Chinatown Madame and now an independently wealthy artist and art dealer, was invited by Mrs. Hopkins to stay with her, and now it was the entire Shortridge family who lived with the widow. These were hard times, as the strikes were on at the railroads, and high unemployment was the result. The big investors and owners of the machines of progress were not being very kind to the working folks.

Mrs. Hopkins at 68, was becoming senile, and as such, she was probably more conducive to having all these new, live-in guests to watch out for her. Her confusion was humorous to all of the Shortridge family, and Ah Toy, a shrewd businesswoman in her own right, was making a personal effort to make certain the old woman was not being tricked by sly businessmen or local politicians. The late Mark Hopkins, her husband, was one of the four owners of the railroads in the United States, so he left his wife with a vast fortune.

Clara was thankful to be able to have this gigantic mansion for her family to live in. One of the main reasons she had taken the murder case in Chinatown was because they paid her enough so that she could finally bring her family from San Jose to live with her. Now that she was back to plying her daily trade of divorce cases and wills, the money was not as forthcoming as the one hundred dollars per hour she received from the Chinatown Six

Companies during the murder case. One more reason she was grateful to have this abode.

"Carrie, who have you brought home to us?" Ah Toy was mincing her way over the thick Persian carpeting toward them. Clara was still standing with her charge, whose name, she then realized, she did not know. The young woman was staring, fixated would be a better word, at one of the oil paintings hanging on the redwood wall in the living room. Its subject was a female medium in front of the Tin How Temple. The woman in the painting had a crazed, inward stare, and her mouth was open. The Chinese men standing all around her were listening intently to what she was saying. The medium's words, according to the belief, were channeling responses from the Goddess Mazu, who was being carried behind the medium on a colorfully decorated cart.

"She seems to be transfixed by your art, Ah Toy. I found her in this state of somnambulism at my meeting. I think she's been abused by some trauma, and I want your help."

Ah Toy, at age fifty-eight, was still a beautiful woman. She wore a long black silk dress called a *cheongsam* that extended down to cover her bound feet, and her hair was still mostly black, although waves of gray were present, and her temples were completely white. She minced over to stand beside the young woman. The living room in this Victorian mansion resembled an art gallery rather than a place to entertain guests. Long mahogany benches faced the walls, which were filled with hundreds of oils, watercolors and sculpted designs on wooden platforms. Mrs. Hopkins was one of the biggest art collectors in the United States.

"Why are you fascinated by this piece, my dear?"

8

Ah Toy whispered to the girl. The older woman knew immediately not to burst out in her usually flamboyant voice. The former Chinatown Madame had worked with thousands of fragile young women, and she knew how to handle a damaged psyche. She had been successful in the sex trade because she was gentle, and she had used a woman's beauty and her more mysterious qualities to please men rather than overt and animalistic sexual intercourse.

"I can do this," the girl said, matter-of-factly.

"Do what? What's your name? I am Ah Toy."

Clara listened intently to the conversation. Her detective abilities were on alert, as she sensed there would be an interesting exchange.

"Adeline Quantrill. I can speak in the voices from beyond." Adeline touched her red lips with the tips of the fingers of her right hand. Her face was pretty, oval and Asian-looking, although her eyes were not slanted. It was her jet-black hair and dark eyes beneath the brushes of eyebrows that made her appear Oriental. Her breathing was now regular, and she seemed to be responding well to Ah Toy's questions.

"Beyond. Do you mean voices from our departed souls? Our relatives and friends who've passed on?"

"No. I mean voices from those who are not willing to share what they're thinking to others. Some are dead, but others are alive. They exist in prisons made by men and in prisons created by the mind."

"I see. That's quite a magnificent gift you have! I want to learn more." Ah Toy encircled the girl's shoulders with her arm.

"I found her crying. She told me she was at some kind of trial. The attorneys would not listen to her. She

9

said they kept arguing about what the witnesses had testified. Also, she said that somebody was still out there—a man." Clara stepped over to stand next to her friend.

Adeline pulled away, and her snub nose wrinkled, her mouth turned down, her head began to slowly shake, from side-to-side, and she began to flash her teeth like a caged cat. The voice that came out of her diaphragm was not that of a teenaged young woman, however, it was the deep baritone of a tortured male.

"They come to me like lost sheep. I attract them with my recipes for sexual fulfillment, you see. The energies of the body can be harvested for a power much greater than the power men have over them! I can teach them the joys of producing passion as it's linked to the dead. Intercourse with their husbands only leads to death. But intercourse with me leads to the release of the soul into a new realm of power on Earth!"

Ah Toy spoke gently to the possessed woman. "Who are you? Why do you have such power?"

Adeline did not look at Ah Toy. She continued to stare, flaring her nostrils and flashing her teeth. "I am a follower of Dr. Paschal Beverly Randolph. He taught me the gift of animal magnetism before he killed himself in Ohio. Now I have perfected his teachings, and women can at last learn the only way to free themselves from the slavery over their minds and bodies."

Clara was intrigued. Most of her abolitionist and suffragist work had been "allowed" because the Spiritualist Movement, of which Dr. Randolph was a member, gave women a voice that they would not have had otherwise. The male patriarchy forbade most women from speaking in public, and women themselves were fighting the equal rights suffragists because they believed gaining more political power would lead to the same corruption that men had created.

However, Clara and her sisters still spoke out for the rights of women because they knew it was the only truly political path toward ultimate equality under the law. If they had to speak as if they were "possessed" by some otherworldly spirit, so be it. They would speak wherever they could to get their message out to others. But this young woman seemed to be speaking about something more sinister afoot. Dr. Randolph had been a controversial practitioner, and some said his combination of sex and power led to lascivious cravings and ungodly rituals inside the bedroom. Could Adeline be a victim of such practices?

"But how can these women free themselves?" Clara asked the inevitable question.

For the first time, the girl turned toward the voice and stared at Clara. Her masculine voice became a harsh whisper, and what she then said chilled Clara's mind as if this man were in the room and had addressed her personally. She knew after it was said that it was leading her into a morass of dark sexual practices, and the visitation of urges that she thought were only present in men who were engaging in bloody and horrendous warfare.

"They release the souls of their husbands, of course!" The voice said.

Chapter 2: The Clairvoyant

The Hopkins Mansion, One Nob Hill, San Francisco, May 2, 1886

When the girl came out of her trance, Clara knew she had to act. If Adeline were ill, then she needed medical attention. If she were somehow telling them the truth, then another course of action must be taken. As an attorney, Clara Foltz understood the importance of memory. In her trial experience as a defense lawyer, she knew how to ask the questions that would demonstrate flaws in memory. This young woman needed to be questioned to determine her ability to tell the truth about her experiences.

"Adeline, are you aware of the voice that just came forth from your body?" Clara took the girl's hands into her own and gazed into her eyes. Her pupils were no longer pinpoints. They looked normal. Perhaps hysteria had caused the affect seen in the meeting house on Clay Street.

"Voice? What voice, Madam?" The girl cocked her head to the side and smiled. "If I speak, it is with my own voice. If some other sound came from me, I would remember. You see, Mum, I remember every moment of my life since I was eight years of age."

Ah Toy sat down on the other side of the girl on the long bench. "Carrie, we must test her. I have seen this

12

before in one of my girls. When she got off the steamship, I was able to procure her before the Tongs sold her off to the sex slave trade. Yes, her name comes to me. Liu Chunhua. She could recall every day she had lived beginning back at her village in Guangdong province. She would tell me what was occurring at the exact date and hour—not just her personal experience, but also about those people and events around her. She told me she had two moving pictures in her mind. One was her sight and experience of the present, and the other was the immense pictorial history of her past. She had the ability to order her imagistic memories as one would organize one's closet of clothes and shoes. Come to think of it, she was very orderly in her personal habits as well."

"We have something more important to contend with here. This girl has been privy to murder. She told me about being at a trial where the lawyers ignored her testimony. Isn't that correct, Adeline?" Clara touched the girl's arm.

"I know every word that was said that day. I can tell you what each witness was saying, and I can tell you what the lawyers asked them. Would it help if I gave you their stories about the murder?" For the first time, the girl's face seemed to become animated with something close to joy. It was as if her ability to recite what she remembered was a channel to a personal type of pleasure.

"I certainly want to hear more about this case. What about you, Ah Toy? Do you think Adeline's ability can serve to explore this rather macabre event further? Perhaps we can even discover why Adeline believes she knows who the murderer is."

Ah Toy nodded. "Of course, we have no direct method of verifying the authenticity of her memories. I could do so with Chunhua because she kept diaries of her daily activities in China."

"I keep a diary too! I began keeping it after my parents were killed by renegade Chiricahua Apaches two miles outside Tombstone, Arizona, on April 16, 1876, at ten fifty-two AM, when I was eight years and three months old. After they died, I knew I was going to be alone the rest of my life. We were coming out West from New York City, to seek our fortunes, and our train was attacked. Mother and Father were killed with a hatchet by one of the intruders. A Pinkerton guard shot all five of them before they could kill more passengers. I was placed in the Methodist orphanage when we arrived in San Francisco, and that's when I began keeping my diary. I wanted to remember everything from before, and I wanted to remember everything in my new life alone. It's been the only way I can cope with the daily memories and organize them to fit my personal puzzle."

"Good God! Do you have any relatives in San Francisco or perhaps in New York?" Clara was concerned for the young woman's safety and mental health.

"Just a maiden aunt in New York. She has twelve cats and no children, so I am on my own, for the most part. I have been cared for by the Rosicrucians, however, after I turned eighteen."

"This was where you got involved with the alleged murder?"

When Clara said the word "murder," the girl winced and drew back.

"Yes, but the others were very kind to me. It was when *he* came to the meeting that I became involved. There is one problem about all of this, however."

14

"And what is that?" Clara leaned forward.

"Although I can remember what he said and what he promised us, I cannot, for the life of me, remember what he looks like or what his name is. Isn't that odd?"

Ah Toy stared at Clara. "I would expect perhaps some kind of mesmerizing influence. I have seen it done. One of my ladies wanted to forget a trauma she experienced with a client, and a doctor was able to hypnotize her so that she forgot it completely."

"No court of law would accept such evidence," Clara said. "It's quite difficult to prove this is scientifically possible under strictly controlled conditions. For example, this possession of Adeline's. She may have had a traumatic experience whereby she can now mimic the voice she heard, but I doubt it was caused by spirit possession or hypnotic means."

"Let's start the test to see if she has this autobiographical memory," Ah Toy said. "I propose we use a *Farmer's Almanac*. I believe Mrs. Hopkins has one in the Study. It has all the weather conditions recorded for the past years. Chunhua was able to tell me the correct forecast, using the exact dates and times when the weather changed."

"I shall retrieve it. Your bound feet are quite a hindrance when speed is a necessity." Clara got up from the bench and hurried off to the next room, turning right at the front door.

When she returned, she held a mammoth, quite dusty tome in both of her hands. She set it down with a grunt on the bench and began turning pages.

"All right. Meteorology. Which date should I choose?"

"Choose a date that may have a strange occurrence," Ah Toy suggested.

"Here's a good date. April 20 and 21, 1880. What was the weather like in Napa Valley and in San Francisco?"

Adeline moved her forefinger in the air, as if she were turning invisible pages. "It was the greatest rainfall in recorded history. I mean, since 1850, when these weather conditions began to be recorded."

"No need for egotistical levity, young lady," Clara smiled. "What were these grand totals?"

"San Francisco had three and two-tenths inches in twenty-four hours. Oh, and Napa Valley had a quite remarkable fourteen and seven-tenths inches. We had to place burlap bags filled with sand all around the doors of the orphanage on Sutter Street. We could go nowhere for the entire week it was so stormy."

Clara raised her eyebrows. "She's quite correct. Exactly what it says here, to the decimal!"

Both women questioned the girl for an hour about a variety of events and phenomenon occurring in the past, and Adeline was able to answer them all with complete accuracy. She even added personal comments about what she was doing that day, such as what she ate and with whom she socialized.

Clara knew it was time to get Adeline's story about the trial. Even if her testimony today could not be used in a court of law, the attorney believed, it may lead to clues which might assist them in their hunt for this phantom doctor and possible murderer. When Adeline spoke in this doctor's voice, what was said made Clara's flesh crawl. There was something about the logic and tone of the words which were innately dangerous. Clara knew she also needed to read more about this doctor's mentor, Dr. Paschal Beverly Randolph. All she knew was that one of the books he wrote, *Magia Sexualis*, was banned from distribution by the United States Postal Service. Therefore, this student of his must have obtained a copy of it secretly from the master himself.

"Carrie! Pay attention! Adeline just slumped over. Her face is pale. I think she may have fainted." Ah Toy raised the girl's torso and slapped her cheeks gently. "Adeline, wake up! Are you ill?"

"She must be starving. It's time for dinner anyway," Clara said, looking at the grandfather clock standing next to a statue of Mark Hopkins, Mary's late husband. "I'll call the children, and you get Mrs. Hopkins. We'll continue this after we eat."

"Yes, I believe you're right. When you mentioned food, she woke up. I'll go tell Hannigan to prepare another setting, and then I'll get the old woman." Ah Toy stood up and began mincing her way out of the huge living room on the ground floor of the mansion. Clara guided Adeline toward the dining room, which was connected to the living room on the east end.

***

The dining room table seats were filled with all five of Clara's children and her two parents, Elias and Telitha Shortridge. For the first time in over a year, the attorney and detective had her family together. The kind owner of the Hopkins Victorian mansion, Mary Hopkins, sat at the head of the table. She was beaming at all these guests of hers, as if she were the queen of a fantasy realm. Her dementia, in fact, was creating within her mind a splendid assortment of dubious realities that Clara and her family enjoyed immensely.

17

When Ah Toy escorted Adeline Quantrill into the room, everybody became silent and stared at her. In her usual, polite manner, the former Chinatown Madame introduced the newcomer to the gathered family.

"My friends, this is Adeline Quantrill. She has quite a unique ability I am certain you will all find interesting and entertaining. At the moment, however, she is also famished."

The eighteen-year-old plopped down into a high-back mahogany chair, as she could no longer stand.

Ah Toy pointed to each of the family members around the table. "Mister Elias Willets Shortridge is the elder of our group. He is Clara's father, and he is also a lawyer and pastor. He presently assists his daughter with her legal practice and saves souls on the weekends."

Elias was wearing his usual blue suit and vest with a gold pocket watch dangling from his vest pocket. He was a balding man with a thick gray mustache, and he nodded at the girl and pushed forward a cane that was balanced against his chair. "Infirmity of age keeps me from keeping up with my daughter, and, most especially, these wild animals called my grandchildren. I shall endeavor soon to cage them and sell them to the passing circus if they don't soon become tamed. I am very pleased to make your acquaintance, young lady."

Adeline gazed at the elder Shortridge, and then smiled. "I see you're a Campbellite Christian, dear sir. Have you baptized your adult children unto their remission of sins?"

The sixty-one-year-old man was taken aback by this girl's knowledge of his religion. "Why, of course I have! There can be no salvation unless the adult is submerged by an authentic Campbellite minister. The

Millennium of Christ's return is being ushered in by our reformation baptisms."

"How did you know my father was a Campbellite? I never told you anything about my family." Clara frowned at the young girl. "Who are you? How did you find out about him?"

Adeline whipped her head back and forth until her auburn curls broke from their bun and slashed against her shoulders. "No, good sir! Jesus never baptized a single one of his apostles. How can you claim such power over your flock?" She laughed, and then the voice of the phantom minister returned to her, and she bellowed, "Let me have these lovelies! I will teach them how to restore the power they had before Eve. They can become Lilith, controlling the sex act, and reaping what was stolen from them by your false Yahweh!" The girl's gray eyes flashed as she moved her head to stare, in turn, at each of the adult women at the table, including Mrs. Shortridge. She pointed her right forefinger at each one and mumbled what sounded like the same gibberish Clara and Ah Toy had heard earlier.

The sound was so frightening that Virginia Knox, ten, and David Milton, fifteen, got up from their seats and rushed over to stand beside their grandfather to protect him from this possessed young woman. "Grand, you must not allow her to stay here!" David said, frowning.

"I must tell you all. When Adeline becomes agitated and speaks in this deep voice, she has no memory of it afterward." Clara tried to think of a way she could explain it to the younger children. "She is making believe she is somebody else, but she cannot remember it when she's finished pretending. We're going to try to help her with this."

"Do you truly not know what you just said?" Samuel Cortland, eighteen, who was seated next to Adeline at the table, was sharing his mother's intellectual curiosity. He straightened his red silk bow tie. "What is it you feel inside?"

Adeline was watching two of the female servants pouring out soup into the bowls with a large ladle. "May I have some of that?" She licked her lips and pointed.

"Of course, my dear! Sophie, pour some soup for Adeline," Mrs. Hopkins instructed the servant. "Do you do any other impressions? Your Grover Cleveland was quite good! Of course, you're not as rotund."

"I can't understand why Ah Toy believes Mrs. Hopkins is losing her memory. She obviously knows who the president is." Trella Evelyn, twenty, was always defending the eldest owner of their new home. Trella was wearing a Suffragette dress, a long purple affair with a matching necktie draped down the center of her white blouse, and a medium bustle in the back.

"I am sorry, but you didn't answer my question, Adeline," Samuel said.

"Yes, why don't you respond? Perhaps she's the daft one at this table," sixteen-year-old Bertha May said, tucking a cloth napkin inside her high collar to protect her frilly blouse before picking up her spoon.

"She is quite daft! She has bats in her belfry!" Little Virginia squealed.

"Calm down, right now! Let the girl respond," said the sixty-two-year-old grandmother, Talitha Shortridge, from the other side of the table.

The noise was bothering the young woman, and she stopped eating the soup to cover her ears with her hands. She began the humming that Clara had heard her do before at the meeting house and on the cable car.

"Silence! We must all show some respect for this young medium." Ah Toy said, raising her right hand. "Some persons are gifted with the ability to channel the voices from the spirit world. Adeline has this skill, and we must learn from her."

Samuel, who was still staring fixedly at the girl, gradually became her center of attention. Adeline lowered her hands from her ears, turned her head to the left where he sat, and she smiled at him.

"Feel inside? I feel humbled at being allowed at your fine table. What a glorious family you have!" Adeline picked up her spoon again and dipped it into her bowl. "And this tomato soup is like drinking the warm blood from Zeus's lips!" Adeline's white teeth were covered in the red liquid.

"How ghastly!" Virginia's face wrinkled into a prune.

"She's using a metaphor, Clara Virginia," her mother said, using her private name for her youngest. "Children, what is a metaphor of speech?"

All the children's eyes rolled with displeasure in their thinking heads, but only Trella answered. "A metaphor is an image that takes the place of another, more common image, to show a startling comparison. We are obviously not really slurping the blood of the Greek god Zeus, but the image seems to compare our tomato soup with the nectar of the gods."

As if on cue, Samuel, Bertha, Virginia and David began to loudly slurp their soup.

"Enough!" Talitha shouted. "We shall finish our dinner, and then discuss what we can do to help your mother with this young woman."

THE SPIRITUALIST MURDERS

***

Ah Toy decided that the Library was the best room to work with Adeline. Therefore, after dinner, all members of the family over the age of eighteen adjourned to watch her question the young woman. Ah Toy sat at the large table for reading the newspapers and magazines, and the young medium sat next to her. Ah Toy instructed everyone else to stay at least ten feet from where she was, so the rest of the family settled into soft reading chairs from Europe and antique divans from Asia.

This was a library created for one of the wealthiest women in America. It contained over 3,000 volumes, all classified and categorized under the Dewy Decimal System. Ah Toy and the children were able to improve their language skills and locate information for their school work. The Chinese artist and teacher thought it was a fitting location to balance yin and yang and to delve into the mind of a young spiritualist medium. It was a place where the mind and the spirit could meet.

"Adeline, you said you can go back to that trial and repeat exactly what was said by each witness. How many witnesses were there? Also, you stated that your testimony was ignored by the court. Why was that?" Ah Toy kept the tone of her voice calm and reflective. She knew that any aggressiveness or perceived threat on her part could prevent the girl's responses from coming forth.

"There were three witnesses, not including myself. My testimony was ignored because the judge believed me to be mentally deranged. He said I was not capable of sound recollection." Adeline looked down at her hands and then raised her head and stared into Ah Toy's dark eyes. "I was the only one who saw an actual murder take place, but I was not allowed to speak."

"Were they aware of your special talents of recollection?" Clara asked. She was sitting in a chair at the table next to Ah Toy.

"The judge said because I was sixteen, and because I had suffered from so much trauma, he didn't deem it proper for me to speak about matters of evidence."

"But, you were an eyewitness to a murder. Certainly somebody, especially the prosecution, would have listened to you." Clara sounded impatient.

Ah Toy raised her right forefinger to her lips. "Did you speak in one of your voices to any of these court attorneys or to the judge?" Ah Toy wanted to get deeper into the young woman's psyche.

"Yes! It was May 2, 1884, in the court of Judge Holland Wentworth. I was called to the witness stand by the Prosecutor, District Attorney Matthew C. Welles, Jr. at exactly ten minutes after three in the afternoon. I was told before the trial by Mr. Welles that he was going to ask me about what I had seen Dr. McCauley do to the accused, Mrs. Rachel Wilson-Rafferty, at the Rosicrucian Hall. He never asked me about the murder. He just wanted me to tell the court about how Dr. Adam McCauley hypnotized his subjects, as he called them."

"What went wrong?" Ah Toy raised her eyebrows. "Is that why you channeled the voice? Were you angry because they would not listen to you?"

"I never remember what happens after I do it. However, the judge informed me that I was speaking in a male's voice on the witness stand. Even though the other three women screamed when they recognized it, nobody in the court believed I could become a voice from the past." Adeline smiled. "But you believe me, don't you?"

Ah Toy returned the smile. "Yes, my dear. Tell me. What did Dr. McCauley do when he heard you imitate this voice?"

"He smiled. And then he whispered something to Rachel's attorney, Miss Laura de Force Gordon. Dr. McCauley was testifying for her at the trial."

"Laura Gordon? She was defending Rachel Rafferty? She's one of my dearest friends and fellow attorneys. We argued a murder case against each other, and we also worked to get the law passed in California which allowed women to become attorneys and attend law school. It seems that this McCauley could be a possible suspect. I want to talk with Laura about this," Clara said.

"I believe it's a good time to have you channel the testimony of these three witnesses. We shall begin with the first woman. Please, before you go into your trance, tell us the name of this woman and how she knew Dr. McCauley." Ah Toy's eyebrows furrowed in concentration. "Carrie, do you have anything to add?"

"I would also like to know what Adeline observed about these three witnesses. I would assume they were testifying about what was done by Dr. McCauley to Rachel Rafferty, was it not?" Clara leaned her chin forward into the cradle made by her hands. "Was Miss Gordon trying to show that her client Rachel could have been mesmerized by McCauley?"

"Yes, they had all observed the hypnosis which Dr. McCauley used upon the defendant, Mrs. Rachel Wilson-Rafferty. Each one had a different perception about what had occurred. This was what caused the attorneys to get angry. Of course, nobody cared about what I saw. Most importantly, nobody cared that I actually witnessed the result of Dr. McCauley's hypnosis. I saw …" Again,

Adeline began sobbing into her hands.

"Did you see the murder of Mr. Rafferty?" Clara asked.

Adeline stared at the attorney and paused, as if she were remembering something. "Yes. I was working for the victim, Mr. Brian Rafferty, at his home in Pacific Heights. I was the upstairs maid, and on the night of April 3, 1884, I witnessed his wife, Rachel, kill him during their sexual union."

"My goodness! You could have sent that woman go the gallows." Elias said from his seat on the divan.

Ah Toy instinctively knew it was not that simple. "Did anybody in that courtroom believe Rachel was hypnotized by Dr. McCauley to kill her husband?"

"No, of course not! The good doctor was testifying for the defense. He was saying that he knew Mrs. Rafferty was too mentally imbalanced to know if what she was doing was right or wrong. The jury believed it. Women were not capable of the hatred required to commit such murders. Especially of their husbands, who were their sole providers and masters of the house." Adeline wiped tears from her cheeks. "However, I saw her do it, and I could also hear what she was thinking."

"Do you mean to say you are also a telepathist?" Clara asked. "Can you read people's minds as well as recall what they said?"

The young woman laughed. "Of course. It's my curse." She turned to gaze over at Samuel, who was fidgeting while seated upon an old red chair with fringes on the sides and a lace doily on the headrest. "For example, Samuel is now thinking he wants to leave and go play billiards with his friends."

"That's not difficult to discern," Samuel shook his

head. "She saw I was uncomfortable, and most young men enjoy billiards. What are my two friends' names then? If you are truly clairvoyant, then you should know that as well."

"One is named Roger. Roger Dowdy. The other's name is Ezra Levine."

There was a dead silence for several minutes. Telitha Shortridge finally stood up and walked solemnly over to the girl. She placed her wrinkled hand on Adeline's shoulder. The girl looked up and gazed into the older woman's face. Telitha told her, "You shall never mention this ability of yours to any living soul outside this family. Do you hear me, young lady?"

"I shall not, Mrs. Shortridge. I have read about what happens to people like me."

"You have? You mean, like what happened in Nathaniel Hawthorne's tale? 'Young Goodman Brown'?" Trella Evelyn asked.

"No, we are now too civilized to kill people for being witches. I once asked Mrs. Young, who was our house mistress at the orphanage, why she was thinking about how attractive the priest, Father O'Shaughnessy was, as he could not return her affection. She became quite enraged, and she shouted at me that they put people like me in the insane asylum. She then picked-up a screwdriver and held the flathead against my temple. She said the doctor would drive a hole into my brain until I could no longer think evil thoughts. She said I was cursed by the Devil."

"Are your prognostications correct one hundred percent of the time?" Clara asked.

"No, it seems I can only read the minds of certain people. I don't know why that is, but there are those who seem to send their thoughts to me." Adeline shook her head. I can never predict when it will happen. It just does."

Ah Toy was getting impatient. "All right. Let us hear your channeling of the first witness. It is now obvious that we can get more than what was given at the court. Perhaps we can learn how this Dr. McCauley was able to mesmerize these women so they became his sex slaves."

"Slaves? Aren't you being a bit overly dramatic, Ah Toy? We don't know this doctor was responsible for the murder." Clara frowned at her friend.

Ah Toy turned to her friend and smiled. "Remember that we Asians believe in many more realities than just science and logic. Each of us has been gifted with uniqueness that has nothing to do with our social lives together. It is our connection with the spirit world. Adeline can lead us into this dark realm, but we can never be the masters over such supernatural powers. We can only follow these powers and discover their effect."

"All I want to discover is whether this mesmerist, Dr. McCauley, has the power to train wives to kill their husbands. If so, then it is he who should go on trial and perhaps be placed into a mental hospital. But we need incontrovertible evidence, beyond any reasonable doubt. At the present, I have many such doubts." Clara cleared her throat. "Please, Adeline, you may now take us back to that day in the courtroom. It would seem we have a lot to learn."

Ah Toy had few arguments with her best friend, but this was an occasion when she had to insist her expertise was to be recognized. She stood up at her seat and addressed the family in a formal voice.

"When I worked in Chinatown as a Madame, there

was a Tong leader of the Hop Sing named Fung Jing Toy. Everyone called him "Little Pete." Little Pete was my uncle. He had the power over the prostitutes that were brought over from southern China to work. Like this Dr. McCauley, my uncle mesmerized women. After he established his power over them, they willingly had sex with strange men."

"What did he tell them? Was it so they could obtain power from having sex with your uncle?" Clara asked.

"No, it wasn't exactly like it was with Dr. McCauley. My uncle told each girl that for every man she had sex with she was gaining dream powers over all men. He would, in fact, get them addicted to opium, and then he would take them to private orgies in the Palace Hotel. He charged the white men a lot of money to participate in these bacchanals. The girls were under his complete control, and my uncle soon became known in the masculine circles as the 'King of Chinatown.' As far as I know, he is still plying his illegal trade, and he even has a white body guard. Mr. C. H. Hunter. My uncle reasoned that no rival Tong would risk killing a white man." Ah Toy sat back down and folded her hands into the lap of her silk *cheongsam*.

"You never told me this," Clara said. "However, I believe your Uncle Pete may be able to assist us when we attempt to confront this Dr. McCauley. Thank you, Ah Toy, for your candid honesty."

"I am always here to extend the patterns of connections between dark and light. Just as your lover, Captain Lees, uses the Tongs as informers to catch other criminals, I also believe the dark side can aide the powers of light." Ah Toy raised her hand. "Shall we begin? Adeline, please favor us with your powers of spiritualism."

***

Pre-order this new mystery in the Portia of the Pacific series.
Available at Amazon and Kobo.
You can also join the author's mailing list.

ABOUT THE AUTHOR

James Musgrave's work has been recently featured in *Best New Writing 2011*, Eric Hoffer Book Awards, Hopewell Press, Titusville, N.J. He was semi-finalist in the Black River Chapbook Competition, Fall, 2012. He was also in a Bram Stoker Award Finalist volume of horror fiction, *Beneath the Surface, 13 Shocking Tales of Terror*, Shroud Publishing, San Francisco, CA. His historical mystery series starring Detective Patrick James O'Malley was selected as "featured titles" by the American Library Association's Self-E Program for Independent Authors. The first mystery in that series, *Forevermore*, won the First Place blue ribbon for Best Historical Mystery, in the Chanticleer International Clue Book Awards, 2013. James lives in San Diego, and is the publisher of EMRE Publishing, LLC.

84599575R00137

Made in the USA
Middletown, DE
21 August 2018